Frederick J. Jobson

A Tribute to the Memory of the Rev. Jabez Bunting

SALZWASSER VERLAG

Frederick J. Jobson

A Tribute to the Memory of the Rev. Jabez Bunting

Reprint of the original, first published in 1859.

1st Edition 2022 | ISBN: 978-3-37512-669-8

Verlag (Publisher): Salzwasser Verlag GmbH, Zeilweg 44, 60439 Frankfurt, Deutschland
Vertretungsberechtigt (Authorized to represent): E. Roepke, Zeilweg 44, 60439 Frankfurt, Deutschland
Druck (Print): Books on Demand GmbH, In de Tarpen 42, 22848 Norderstedt, Deutschland

A TRIBUTE

TO THE MEMORY OF THE

REV. JABEZ BUNTING, D.D.

THE SERVANT OF HIS GENERATION.

A TRIBUTE

TO THE MEMORY OF THE

REV. JABEZ BUNTING, D.D.:

BEING A SERMON PREACHED ON THE OCCASION OF HIS DEATH, IN EASTBROOK CHAPEL, BRADFORD, YORKSHIRE, JULY 18TH, 1858:

WITH

A SKETCH

OF HIS

CHARACTER AND SERVICES.

BY

FREDERICK J. JOBSON, D.D.

LONDON:
HAMILTON, ADAMS, AND CO.;
SOLD BY JOHN MASON, 14, CITY-ROAD,
AND 66, PATERNOSTER-ROW.

1858.

To the

REV. WILLIAM MACLARDIE BUNTING.

My dear Sir,

When the deep grave in the Methodist Cemetery of City Road, London, had closed upon the mortal remains of your honoured father,—and I looked around for one who should henceforward represent among us his name and house,—my mind, with the minds of thousands, glanced immediately towards you. And now, when I have before me, for publication, my humble tribute to his great memory; and when I seek for one who shall be able to attest the substantial truth of what it contains, and who, while perceiving its manifold imperfections in form and manner, shall, in the strength of affection for the deceased, and in the generosity of a noble nature, kindly appreciate my motives,—I cannot find any person so fully answering all my wishes as yourself.

Allow, then, this public presentation to you of an unworthy record of your father's virtues; and accept it as from one whose happiness it was to witness the perpetual spring of joy which that father possessed in having a son of refined intelligence, and of devout evangelical faithfulness, so honourably associated with him in the holy ministry,—a son on whose deep reverence and devoted love he could surely lean, as he descended by slow and gentle steps to the grave.

With sentiments of unfeigned respect and affection, I am ever,

"Thine own friend, and
thy father's friend,"
FREDERICK JAMES JOBSON.

QUEEN STREET CHAPEL,
HUDDERSFIELD, *November*, 1858.

Prefatory Notice.

REVERENCE and love for Dr. Bunting, whose intimate friendship it was my privilege to enjoy, rendered the retracing of his character and labours a relief to my mind under the heavy sense of the loss I had sustained by his death. As the minister of a loving people who revered his name, and whom, in the course of Methodist itinerancy, I was about to leave for another sphere of labour, I was thus ready at their request to improve the event of Dr. Bunting's death publicly with them. At their request, also, I print what was delivered to them. One thought, if it had been allowed full weight, would have prevented me doing so,—the consciousness of an inadequate and unworthy representation of my subject. Other considerations might have had the like tendency; namely, that more deserving memorials have been already raised to the departed great one by abler and more experienced hands; as well as the announcement formally made that, in due time, a full memoir of him is to be supplied to the world by his own gifted son, Mr. Percival Bunting, of Manchester. There is, for instance, the graphic sketch of him by the Rev. William Arthur, first inserted in the "Christian Times" newspaper. There is the Presidential portraiture of him, effectively set forth by the Rev. Francis A. West before the Irish Conference, in Dublin, and copied for us in our weekly journal. And since my discourse was delivered, there have been published, not only the admirable Funeral Sermon preached for him by the Rev. Thomas Jackson in City Road Chapel, London, but also, officially in the "Minutes of Conference," the just and discriminating character of him from the pen of the Rev. Isaac Keeling. But, bereft as I have been, by his death, of a father and a friend,—and feeling that there is, for me, henceforth in life a vacancy which can never be filled,—I cannot, with all these honourable memorials of him in view, deny myself the melancholy gratification of rearing my own slender column to so beloved a memory; and I pray, while I do so, that my imperfect labour may be in some degree promotive of the Divine glory.

To all acquainted with the disturbing influences and cares accompanying a Methodist minister's removal from one Circuit to another, I need not apologize for the delay which has occurred in committing the following pages to the press.

F. J. J.

SERMON.

"For David, after he had served his own generation by the will of God, fell on sleep, and was laid unto his fathers, and saw corruption."—Acts xiii. 36.

How different are the reflections produced in the minds of the living by the departure from earth of the righteous and the wicked; and how different are the feelings with which we contemplate the spiritual and eternal condition of the one and of the other! Is it one of the gay, thoughtless lovers of earthly pleasure who has departed this life?—one whose entrance into company was the sure signal for mutual congratulations and rejoicings, and whose presence was accounted full and certain security from weariness and dulness? Is he dead,—the life of the evening party,—the pride of the festive scene?—he who was wont to kindle laughter among his companions, and to keep the table in a roar? Then you must not make more than a distant allusion to his name among his surviving companions; for he has gone from their companionship to the dark house of the grave, where the worm is feeding upon him; and there are remembrances of ill-spent time and talents that but ill consort with the final account he has to render before God, and with his eternal state. The thought of his death brings a skeleton into his vacant place at their feasts: his volatile and jovial character they cannot bear to think upon with the serious fact before them that he is now in the world of spirits; and therefore they shun his memory.

Or suppose the departed heritor of humanity has been one who devoted himself to worldly and selfish objects; who gave himself to the ceaseless pursuit of hard grinding gain; who was the leader in the market; who doubled his riches over and over again during his life-time; who got all he could, kept all he got, and closed his heart against all appeals made to him for charity and benevolence? Is he—the man of wealth and of the world—dead? Then you will find that they who knew him converse sparingly and hastily concerning him; and that when they have summed up his worth in riches, they pass from the mention of him to the inheritors of his fortune. They do not attempt to carry the account concerning him further; for it will not bear investigation and reflection.

And then again in relation to the man of mere morality and external virtue,—while his friends dwell for a few moments with seeming complacency on the daily routine of his existence, and speak of its regularity and order,—how soon they come to a standstill, a sort of paralysis of speech! and their looks, coupled with their serious silence, proclaim to you that their attempt at praise has been a consciously lame apology for the want of real spirituality in the man, and that they have at heart an appalling fear that all is not well with him in the eternal world.

But how different the feelings and sentiments of survivors at the death of good and faithful servants of the Lord, who lived for the glory of God and the welfare of mankind! Their death is not a subject to be shunned. The remembrance is not painful, either of their life on earth, or of their state in the spiritual world. Is it the devoted, laborious, useful Christian who is dead? Then no one of his friends speaks of him with bated breath, or whispers his name in a corner, as if afraid to mention it. He may be spoken of with the tear of affection, but it will be also with the kindling smile of holy triumph and rejoicing. So far from shunning his memory, his friends delight to recall it. With pleasure they re-picture the expression of his countenance, they dwell upon the tones of his voice, and especially upon the words he uttered, the truths he maintained, and the deeds he performed; and they are stimulated thereby to imitate his blessed example. If he died young, having been a labourer but for a short time in the vineyard of his Lord, then there is the tender and joyous recollection that he escaped by his short day many trials and sufferings, and went early to his reward. If he lived onward to old age and grey hairs, then there is the more abundant satisfaction in the thought, that he improved his lengthened opportunity for doing good in the world; that he came down to his grave as a shock of corn fully ripe for the heavenly garner, and that he now enjoys the fulness of the saint's reward. If he served his generation by the will of God, and then fell asleep, we think of him with veneration and gratitude; and we associate him in our remembrances with the blessed dead who die in the Lord. Such was the association in the mind of the holy apostle St. Paul, when, referring to David in his sermon at Antioch, he said, "For David, after he had served his own generation by the will of God, fell on sleep, and was laid unto his fathers, and saw corruption."

Such is the difference of men's reflections, whether on an ill-spent or well-spent life of one deceased. But reflection, to be profitable, must not be merely temporary. Indeed, thought does not deserve the name of reflection, if it last but for a few brief moments, and then be dismissed and forgotten. True reflection consists of those weighty and deliberate and often-resumed acts of the mind which impress the heart and influence the will. And our reflections during the service in which we are now engaged ought to lead to self-application. We are met to commemorate the departure of one who served his generation by the will of God with ability, zeal, and efficiency which few men, in any age, have equalled. And duly to improve the sorrowful event, we ought to think not only of him, but also of the practical lessons which his great example supplies. If we fail to do so, our service, with all its solemnity, will be sinfully defective. If that clear and powerful voice which was heard from this pulpit at the opening of this chapel, were now to speak to us from out the silence of eternity, it would say, "Praise not the dead; but preach for the benefit of the living!" Let us, then, endeavour to improve this event religiously; and, before we proceed to speak of the departed himself, try to learn the Scripture lessons which the text brings home to us.

I. We may observe that it teaches us the great

moral end of man's probationary life: to "serve his generation by the will of God."

II. It presents for our consideration the state of calm and blissful repose which awaits all faithful servants of God at the end of their course,—and that, notwithstanding the inevitable and humiliating circumstances of death and the grave: they "fall on sleep, are laid unto their fathers, and see corruption."

First, then, we are to learn from this passage of Holy Scripture, THE GREAT MORAL END OF MAN'S PROBATIONARY LIFE: he is to "serve his generation by the will of God."

And we are ready to believe that there are few persons so utterly immersed in the cares of the world and in forgetfulness, as to have no passing solicitude for their spiritual position and destiny. Amidst the perpetual whirl of excitement which characterizes our time, there are yet few who have no moments for reflection upon whence they came, what they are doing, and whither they are hastening.

The daily occurrences of life and death, as well as the record of past generations who have lived and died upon the earth, we should say, would prompt to this; for how can beings who know that they are to live hereafter see those who set out with them in the career of life pass one after another from the stage of visible existence, and not reflect at all upon such serious facts? No: thoughtless as mankind are, still there are times when the human spirit enters into its inner chamber, shuts the doors around it, and asks, "What am I? what am I doing here? and why has my lot been cast at this age of the world, and in this part of it?"

Sometimes, when men think of the past, and see how change and ruin have overtaken all things; how the generations of mankind have disappeared and others arisen; how the works of men have perished, populous cities become silent, and the names of many have been obliterated,—they are ready to say, "Of what avail is character, or conduct, during the few days of our continuance in this changeful and dying world? Soon we, too, shall have departed from earth, and be numbered among the forgotten of mankind: let us live for self-gratification and present indulgence: 'Let us eat and drink, for to-morrow we die!'" The record of the text corrects such melancholy and despairing reflections; it teaches us that we have each an important service to perform to our contemporaries,—to the generation of our time. It teaches us that we have a mission from God which invests life with real importance and value. At the same time it presents to us encouraging motives to faithfulness; for the usefulness of holy and benevolent men shall be eternized, not by crumbling marble monuments, but by the imperishable results of the benefits they have conferred upon mankind. It teaches us that we are not a race of isolated and independent beings, sent to live a while on the earth without an object and without a mission; but that we have each our place and sphere of action, as well as the time of our life and labours, assigned us by Divine Providence; that, like John the Baptist, we have to fulfil our course; like David, we have to serve our own generation by the will of God; and that, like Christ, we have to work the works of Him that sent us, and to finish the work He has given us to do.

And this is, indeed, a powerful reflection, when it fully possesses and fills the mind. It impresses men with the conviction of the true use of life, and with the fact of its great responsibility. It teaches man that he has not come into existence by chance, and fallen into his position by accident; but by the direct and immediate appointment of God. It teaches him that the religion which he is to have and to manifest is not one which is selfish, but which is benevolent and serviceable to mankind. It does not unfold the religion of a recluse in the desert, or in the monastery; but the religion that shall be effective in the home-dwelling, in the street, and in the market-place. It does not present to us the picture of a sickly, tender flower, which must be set in a nook and sheltered in a corner, lest it should fade in the sun or fall in the breeze; but a hardy, healthful plant, that shall bear the storms and heat of life. It does not set before us a religion which shuns the world because sinners are there, but which goes into the highways and hedges to find them and compel them to come in: a religion which goes about doing good, and which seeks to save them that are lost. It does not recommend to us a religion which employs itself only in building sepulchres for the dead of past generations, or in drawing out fanciful schemes for the use of future generations, but which serves its *own* generation by the will of God.

In a wide and extensive sense, "our own generation" may be viewed as an expression comprehending all mankind who are living at the same age and period with ourselves,—all our contemporaries, and that of all parts of the earth. For we are all of one family, having common ties and sympathies. "God has made of one blood all the nations of the earth." And by creating at the first one common father of mankind, God intended that each human being, as he came into life, should feel himself related to all the rest; and that he should have a perpetual consciousness of obligation to promote their welfare. Mankind are to *serve* one another. Not as slaves, in bondage and by compulsion, but freely and voluntarily, and that for each other's benefit. For man to seize his fellow man, bind him in chains, and force him under the lash to serve, is an enormous outrage which God will not fail to punish on that day when He shall make inquisition for blood. We are to be mutually serviceable to each other, and that both for our bodies and our souls; we are to visit and relieve each other in affliction and distress; we are to bear one another's burdens, and so fulfil the law of Christ. And this duty is binding upon all of us, and that without distinction of colour or tribe. The white man is to serve the black man, as well as the black man serve the white man. Indeed, it is in order that we may be mutually helpful to each other that we are placed together in the world at the same time. And such are the fixed and unalterable laws of mutual dependence and influence that, whether as nations or individuals, we must obey these laws, or we cannot prosper. No nation advances in civilization that does not hold intercourse with other nations. No kingdom is prosperous and safe where the several classes stand apart, and at a sullen distance from each other. Trade will not flourish, if the employer and the employed do not serve each other. There is no such thing as absolute independence in the world. Capital must be trusted to circulation, in order to increase; and rich men are as dependent upon the poor for labour as poor men are dependent upon the rich for employment. No family has comfort where the several members are disunited, and refuse to serve each other; and the selfish man who should resolve to stand aloof from his fellow creatures, and never to serve them, must be sadly forgetful of the fact, that he must soon perish, if others were to resolve thus never to serve him. It is *the will of God,* shown by the laws which govern mankind, as well as by the commands and precepts of Holy Scripture, that we should serve our generation.

But the phrase, "served his *own* generation,"

must be understood as having also a more definite and pointed meaning than that of serving mankind at large. David had a special service to perform for Israel,—service for his own generation, —service which he faithfully performed. He had to deliver his generation from the terrors into which the gigantic champion of their enemies threw them, and to free them from the threatened thraldom of their insulting foes. He had to establish them in the worship and service of God, and to reign over them in righteousness. And in all this he so faithfully served that he is described by inspiration as "the man after God's own heart," and is declared to have been perfect, "save in the matter of Uriah the Hittite." For this service he had been fitted and prepared by great natural endowments, and by the unwonted circumstances through which he had passed. Gifted with the highest poetic genius, and having learned gentleness from his flocks, and courage from conflict with the lion and the bear, he was specially qualified to fight with Goliath of the Philistines; to sing such inspired songs that, while he struck the harp with his hand, they should soothe the evil spirit of the king; and to furnish such an opulent treasury of musical thought to his people as should infuse the spirit of harmonious worship among them, and build up the kingdom of Jehovah in Israel. This he did: he served *his own generation* by the will of God.

Not that he served his own generation exclusively; for by what he did for it he has served all succeeding generations of mankind. Who does not bless the name of David, the primal minstrel in the church of God? He is now, as ever, "the sweet singer of Israel." Who has not found the harp of the son of Jesse to soothe him, and to drive away from him the evil spirit? And who has not joyfully employed the Psalmist's joyful words to express before the Lord praises and thanksgivings? Some men, by what they do, not only serve their own generation, but also the generations of mankind in all ages that follow. It was so with the Prophets and Apostles; it was so with the Martyrs and Confessors; it was so with Wycliffe and Luther; it was so with Coverdale and Tyndale, and the other translators of the Bible; it was so with Jewell and Chillingworth, and the other great champions of Protestantism against Popery; it was so with Butler and Paley, and the other great defenders of the truth against infidelity; it was so with John Bunyan and Isaac Watts, who wrote, the one his transcendent "Pilgrim's Progress," and the other his incomparable hymns for little children; it was so with Wesley and Whitefield, and other great active labourers in the vineyard of the Lord; it was so with Howard and Clarkson, with Wilberforce and Buxton, who expended their energies in the great cause of philanthropy; it was so with Jabez Bunting himself. All these were emphatically servants of their own generation; they sought to instruct, to rescue, and to benefit the men of their own age; and still the results of their service run on now, and will run on throughout all time. Not that they laboured ambitiously for posterity, and for their own fame in generations to come. Their commanding, their instant object was in their own day to work for those who were breathing and living around them, and of whose especial wants they were the sympathizing witnesses. Perhaps, their own generation misunderstood and persecuted them. It was so in the case of Columbus, who opened the gates of the Atlantic for the world; it was so in the case of Galileo, who declared the movement of the planetary system; it was so with Harvey, who discerned the circulation of the blood in the human system; and it was so with many other great benefactors of mankind. Yet they proclaimed their discoveries and thus served their own generation, while they left them for the benefit of generations that should follow. They studied, or taught, or toiled, for mankind in their own day; though the influence of what they did extended onwards to the far future. They did their own allotted work, and did not strain after distant projects; they did good as they had opportunity; they worked while it is called to-day; they performed what was immediately assigned them by Divine Providence for the service of mankind.

And we greatly err if we think that any of us have no appointed service to render to our own generation. It is not by chance that we have our lot of existence cast just upon this particular age, and not at some period sooner or later in the progress of time. It is not by accident that we are denizens of this part of the world rather than of any other. Every human being has his ordained life at an especial time, and in an especial place, that he may perform an especial work there and then. To suppose otherwise, would be to suppose that there is less Divine oversight for the intelligent part of creation than for the unintelligent; it would be to conclude that the earth with its order, and beauty, and seasonable fruitfulness, is more under the immediate control and direct government of God than mankind, for whom the earth and its seasons, and its produce, were created and ordained. He ordereth all that is. There is an appointed time to man upon the earth. Our times are in His hands, both as to coming and going; and that whether we die in youth, manhood, or old age. There are no "accidents," strictly speaking, cutting short the life of man. He who observes the fall of every sparrow to the ground has numbered our months and our moments, and fixed the bounds of our life, which we cannot pass. He says to one, "Go," and he goeth; to another, "Come," and he cometh. He setteth the solitary in families: He appoints the bounds of our habitations. He gives us each our station and our work, that we may serve our *own generation* by His will.

And not only so, but every age has its service to be performed, and its servitors. We do not mean that man is the mere creature of circumstances, and that he is made by his age, rather than that his age is marked and impressed by him. Many an age has called for service which has not been rendered: the renderer has not been found. A truly great man, whose name becomes identified with any particular age, goes before his fellows, and does not merely stand abreast with them. It is true there are circumstances favourable to him, which he wields and improves by his superior power: but Luther would never have reformed the Church, nor Wesley have revived religion in this land, if either had waited until the age was considered ready for them. Their own generation was not prepared to receive them: hence the persecution they endured. Enoch and Noah had to perform their peculiar service: they were to be preachers of righteousness to a corrupt generation. Abraham had his peculiar service: he was the depository of Divine truth in an idolatrous generation. Moses and Joshua had their peculiar service: the one to deliver his own generation from the bondage of Egypt, and the other to bring Israel to the promised land. David and Solomon had their peculiar service: it was to exalt the throne and worship of Jehovah among the chosen people. The Prophets had their peculiar service: it was to foretel the coming and the reign of Messiah. Ezra and Nehemiah had their peculiar service: it was to restore the worship of God at Jerusalem after the Captivity. John the Baptist had his peculiar service: it was to herald the glorious advent of the Saviour. The Divine Redeemer had His peculiar service: it was to finish the work which His Father had given Him to do. The Apostles had their peculiar service: it was to preach the Gospel to all nations. The Martyrs had their peculiar service: it was to seal the truth with their blood. Our Lollard and Protestant forefathers in this country had their peculiar service: it was to resist the yoke and break down the pretensions of Rome. Our Puritan forefathers had their peculiar service: it was to break away the lingering attachment to Rome of Laud and his coadjutors. Our fathers in Methodism had their peculiar service: it was to call back Protestantism to its purity, by preaching salvation through faith in Christ, and by enduring persecution, while they employed strenuous efforts to spread scriptural holiness through the land. They had to establish Missions and Schools. And we have our peculiar service: it is to serve our own generation and the times in which we live.

I do not mean that we are to attempt new means and expedients to meet what are described as "the signs of the times." There is, undoubtedly, too great an eagerness to seize upon characteristic features, or upon *what are viewed* as characteristic features of an age, and to shape service to them and for them. Men seem moonstruck with the new forms and phases of society, and demand that the Church shall adapt itself to the said forms and phases. And to hear what is sometimes spoken, inanely and despairingly, of the wants of the age, and of the exhausted power of divinely appointed means, one would suppose that Christianity had become infirm, decrepit, paralytic! The very pulpit must be removed, to give way to the platform; the most grotesque titles for subjects, and the most *outrée* slang phraseology, must be employed in the place of inspired texts of Scripture; and public prayer, as well as praise to God, must be omitted, to take, as it were by guile, the "working classes" of the nation. But human nature in its essential principles, the Gospel of the Son of God in its plainness and simplicity, as a remedy for man's fallen condition, and the necessity of the Holy Spirit's power to save, are the same now as they were eighteen hundred years ago; and the man who shall leave the old paths of usefulness, and shape his means to meet what are said to be "the wants of the times,"—and that under the notion that divinely instituted means for reaching the human heart will not suit the present generation as well as others,—will find, sooner or later, that he has committed a capital blunder.

There is a work which *we* are to work in our day, and which belongs to *us* in the age in which we live. We are not to think that if we had lived in an earlier or later period, or in some other part of the world, or if we had lordly wealth, or leisurely and cushioned retirement, we could more effectually serve our generation. It is in our own present station, condition, and circumstances, that we are appointed to serve mankind. Nor need there be any difficulty in learning what the service required of us is. We have only to consider our relative position, and the wants of our fellow-creatures, to ascertain this. Are you a Minister? Then wait on your ministry.

Are you a teacher? Then wait on your teaching. Are you a master? Then seek the welfare of your servants. Are you a servant? Then serve your master in singleness of your heart, as unto Christ. Are you a parent? Then bring up your children in the nurture and admonition of the Lord. Are you a child? Then love and obey your parents. Are you rich? Then honour the Lord with your substance, and with the first fruits of all your increase. Are you poor? Then be diligent and frugal, and trust in the God of the poor for the supply of all your wants. Are you a member of the Church of Christ? Then consider the spiritual wants of the world: think of Heathenism abroad, and of sin and ignorance at home. Think of the sin of sabbath-breaking. Think how open, shameless, vile intemperance and impurity flaunt themselves in the streets of our metropolis and in the thoroughfares of our principal cities and towns. Think how scepticism and atheism present their front of defiance in London and in our manufacturing towns. Think of the swarms of sensualists and of poor fallen females in every great town of England, Scotland, and Ireland. Think of those moral sinks and moral common sewers, the casinoes, the penny concerts, and the penny gaffs of our great towns. Think of the unevangelized ignorance and low brutality of our multitudinous villages. Think of the sick and the dying poor in the countless alleys, squares, and rows, of our cities and boroughs. Think of the uninstructed, who, in their cellars and attics, would be thankful if experienced Christians would go to them, and read the word of life, and pray with them. Think of Sabbath School, Day School, Tract Distribution, and Benevolent Society institutions. No one who desires to know the will of God in serving his generation can be at a loss to ascertain what that service should be. If any ask sincerely, with Saul of Tarsus, "Lord, what wilt Thou have me to do?" the hand of Providence, the wants of his generation, and the demands of the various enterprises of benevolence and philanthropy before him, will indicate to him the path of duty. And in doing that which God gives him to do, he shall, most surely, see his service crowned with the Divine blessing.

We must, however, have definite principles and rules of action, if we are to become faithful and successful performers of appointed service. We must, for instance, have those definite principles of real religion,—*love to God and love to man.* It is "the generation of the upright" whom God blesses, and whom He employs, instrumentally, to save a "wicked, perverse, and faithless generation." There must be in us that which we recommend others to obtain, or it may be fitly said to us, "Physician, heal thyself!" There must be godly principle to influence and sustain us, or we shall flag and fail in our object. The basis of our action must not be loose, and vague, and floating; if it be, we shall not succeed. If we are to be true and effective workers, we must not be in love with that indefiniteness and latitudinarianism which some so much laud in our day, under the name of "catholicity." Paul would have done little for Christianity, if he had viewed the rationalism of

Athens with indulgence, and had shrunk from denouncing its idolatry. Luther would have done as little as Erasmus for the overthrow of Popery, if he had only timorously recommended that some of its more vulgar excrescences should be removed, and that it should be afresh painted and gilded, instead of lifting the weighty hammer of God's word to break the corrupt idol in pieces. And your own Wesley would have done little, if he had sought, like some men high in the Church in the present times, merely to revive obsolete forms and ceremonies. Men accomplish little if they have not deep convictions of duty. If we are to proclaim truth, we must be clear in our own minds as to what is truth. If the trumpet give an uncertain sound, who shall arm himself for the battle?

Again: there must be *devotedness to duty*. The mind must be supremely set upon one object; and that must be, not to win the honour which comes from man, but to serve our own generation by the will of God. He who runs with two goals in view, runs nowhere: he who aims at two marks, hits neither. There must be oneness of purpose, singleness of eye, purity of motive. The man who cannot labour in the Church without resolutions, "that the thanks of this meeting be given unto him," without notices in the newspapers, or laudations and commendations from those around him, is not the man for sterling usefulness. Honour may come to the devoted servant of God in his course: most probably it will; but he must not seek it primarily: that would unfit him for the Master's use. Like the Son of Man, he is to minister, and not to seek to be ministered unto: he is to become great among his brethren by being the servant of all. The true nobility of disinterestedness and self-forgetfulness distinguishes the men who in sincerity serve their generation by the will of God. Hence the phrase employed in the text to describe David's usefulness literally signifies, to serve as an *under-rower* in a galley. It signifies to take the lowest tier in the bark of his times, and to ply the oar with the arm of one devoted to labour. The reason why there are so many miserable wrecks of character and purpose floating around us, both in the Church and the world, is, that men are not willing to take the place of under-rowers, of servants beneath. They must be on deck for show: they must have hold of the helm, however unfit, and be seen to be in the place of rule and power. It is service, real service, old Methodist service, old Puritan, old Protestant, old Christian service, self-denying service, that is really wanted for the Church in our times; service such as gave to our Methodist forefathers that breadth and weight of character which they possessed, and made them memorable in their usefulness. Not dainty and delicate service, such as some of their children would perform. Not service that picks its steps in the streets, and visits the respectable, and cleanly, and orderly poor,—and such kind of poor only. But service that is not afraid of hail, rain, or snow; that dares to traverse the unswept streets and the filthy alleys, to enter the dusty school-room, to climb the naked garret, or descend the obnoxious cellar, in order to save souls from death. This is the service which, if performed in dependence on God, shall really succeed.

And again: there must be *energy and perseverance*. The hand of the "under-rower" must ply the oar, not only in the calm, but against wind and tide. It is said proverbially, that "the winds and waves are always on the side of the ablest navigators." And it is true that a man of energy usually makes all things, however uncontrollable by others, submit to himself. Everybody knows that the man of decision *will* act; and, knowing this, the crowd opens for him, so that he finds an easy passage where the doubting and timid man can make no way at all. He who fears that a lion is in the path will be sure to find one; but when the man of energy does not see a path open to him by favourable and adventitious circumstances, he cuts it open for himself. "If there were as many devils in the city of Worms as there are tiles on the houses, yet would I go thither," said the lion-hearted Luther, when his friends endeavoured to dissuade him from risking his life before the Emperor and the Pope's Legate, in that city. And he went onward, in spite of opposition and threats, defending and proclaiming the truth, until Protestantism divided Europe against Popery. "Courage, my brother," said valiant old Latimer to his younger fellow-martyr, Ridley, as they were about to be consumed in the flames at Oxford: "we shall this day light up a candle that shall never be extinguished in England!" And his dying prophecy shall be fulfilled. O, for a restoration to the Church of such service as holy Latimer's, and as gallant Luther's! It is energy, it is resolute, determined service, which the Church needs at present; and God send it among us! And not only energetic service, but *persevering* service ought to characterize us. We must ply the oar among the brave-hearted "under-rowers" day by day, and hour by hour. Not one failure, nor a hundred, nor a thousand, must dishearten us. We must toil on amidst all difficulty, all distress, all desertion, all reproach,—looking onward to our heavenly home; for "there is a rest that remaineth for the people of God;" and the prospect of it should hearten us in our labour, and stimulate us to persevere in serving our generation by the will of God.

SECONDLY, then, let us contemplate, as motive for service, THE CALM AND BLISSFUL REPOSE WHICH AWAITS ALL FAITHFUL SERVANTS OF GOD AT THE END OF THEIR COURSE; AND THAT, NOTWITHSTANDING THE INEVITABLE AND HUMILIATING CIRCUMSTANCES OF DEATH AND THE GRAVE: "they fall on sleep, and are laid to their fathers, while their flesh sees corruption."

This peaceful end, and this association with the great and the good, were realized by David when he had served his generation by the will of God, as the Old Testament historians record, (1 Chron. xxix.; 1 Kings ii.,) and as here declared by St. Paul. The scene, as it is described by the Old Testament historians, is thrillingly expressive. David blessed the Lord, and blessed the people; and having his heart's desire in the accession to the throne of his son Solomon, he calmly and peacefully laid himself down in his bed to sleep, after his life of arduous and faithful service; and then they gave him honourable burial with the men of renown, and his flesh saw corruption. Such is the case with all faithful labourers. They can calmly review their life of toil; they do not start back alarmed at the approach of death; they have "no panic" when the last messenger comes; but, like the healthful and satisfied labourer, they lie down in their bed, and fall asleep in Christ; and their friends, venerating their memory, give them honourable burial, and associate them in thought with the great and the good of the spiritual world.

And how significant of their *calm and tranquil repose* at the end of their life, both with regard to the soul and the body, is the emblem of sleep here employed! It may relate, more immediately, to the body sleeping in the grave; for we see a wondrous resemblance between death in its physical aspect and them that sleep in their beds. How often, when viewing the dead in Christ, with the last lingering smile of assured safety still upon the countenance, have we been ready to say, "He is not dead, but sleepeth!" But the term is signally descriptive of the Christian's view of death: it is emphatically the Gospel representation of death. The Lord Jesus Christ has triumphed over death for man; has stripped the grim king of his terrors; and thus to the Christian death is only cessation from suffering and labour: it is sleep, and that upon the Saviour's own bosom. It is not cessation from consciousness, until the resurrection; for there is no such "sleep of the soul" awaiting the servant of God. "To be absent from the body is to be present with the Lord."—"To depart and to be with Christ is far better." There is no interval of suspended life,—not a sand-fall of time,—not an instant between falling asleep in death and waking up to the conscious possession of that inheritance which is "incorruptible, undefiled, and which fadeth not away." To fall asleep, in the meaning of Scripture, is to cease from labour and affliction, from pain and sorrow, and to enter upon eternal rest. Hence Christ said of the brother of Martha and Mary, whom He afterwards declared to be positively dead, "Our friend Lazarus sleepeth." And of Stephen, the first Christian martyr, who sank down into death under stoning from his murderous persecutors, it is said, "He fell asleep." It is the traveller come to the end of his journey, and resting in his heavenly home; it is the mariner escaped from life's storms and tempests, and safe within the unruffled harbour of security and repose; it is the soldier putting off his helmet and corslet, his spear and shield, to rest in peace, free from all the alarums of war. "I heard a voice from heaven," says the holy Apostle, when describing to us what he learned through the open door of Divine revelation, "saying, Write, Blessed are the dead which die in the Lord from henceforth: Yea, saith the Spirit, that they may rest from their labours; and their works do follow them." "There the wicked cease from troubling; and there the weary be at rest."

But who does not perceive that the term "sleep," as applied to the pious dead, is expressive, not only of calm and tranquil repose, but also of *security and confidence?* Men under a sense of insecurity do not lie down to sleep: thought of danger prevents their taking rest in sleep. But to sleep in Christ is to be safe in the keeping of Him who has the keys of hell and death,—of the world of spirits and of the grave: it is to know that none shall pluck them out of His hands; and that "neither death, nor life, nor angels, nor principalities, nor powers, nor things present, nor things to come, nor height, nor depth, nor any other creature, shall be able to separate them from the love of God which is in Christ Jesus our Lord." And who that falls asleep in his bed does not expect to awake again? So believes the Christian,—that he shall awake up in the presence and after the likeness of Christ, and be invested with honour and dignity that shall never pass away. "Them also which sleep in Jesus will God bring with Him." And before they who shall be living upon the earth at the coming of the Saviour shall ascend to meet Him, buried saints shall rise, that they may be caught up together with them in the clouds, to meet the Lord in the air; for "the dead in Christ shall rise first." "We know that, when He shall appear, we shall be like Him: for we shall see Him as He is." "And as we have borne the image of the earthy, we shall also bear the image of the heavenly." Such is the "sure and certain" hope of the servant of the Lord!

The text also speaks of *honourable burial:* "And was laid unto his fathers." David's body was not "cast out," as were the bodies of wicked kings and princes who were not allowed burial in the royal city: these were divided in death from their kindred, because of their crimes. David was "laid unto his fathers." The Scriptures never treat the human body with irreverence, not even when it is forsaken by the living spirit. It is the superlative workmanship of God; with the soul it has been redeemed by Christ; and all creation is represented as groaning and waiting for the redemption of the body. That body, vile in its corruption, shall be raised again incorruptible: it shall come forth from the grave glorious and immortal. Then let it not be "cast out;" but, as in the case of Stephen, let devout men carry it to its burial, and make great lamentation over it. Let it sleep in companionship with its kindred dust,—let it be laid unto its fathers,—let the strong and enduring instinct for burial with our friends be gratified. The Patriarchs of old felt this instinct. Hence Abraham, the father of the faithful, purchased of the sons of Heth "the field of Ephron, which was in Machpelah, which was before Mamre, the field, and the cave which was therein, and all the trees that were in the field, that were in the borders round about, that they might be made sure unto him for a possession of a burying-place." Jacob felt this instinct. He felt it in regard to the members and household connexions of his family. How pathetically he refers to Deborah, Rebekah's nurse, in the place of her burial, and calls the oak which overshadowed her solitary and separate grave, *Allon-bachuth*, "the oak of weeping!" He seemed almost broken-hearted when he related to Joseph how he had to bury Rachel by the road-side, "when there was but a little way to come unto Ephrath." And he felt it still more strongly in regard to himself. He had evidently a dread and a horror of being separated from his kindred in his burial, and of being built up in some cold marble sarcophagus, or under some ponderous pyramid, by the "building masons of Egypt." More than once does he express this feeling to his son Joseph, and that in the most solemn and imploring terms. "If now," said he to him, "I have found grace in thy sight, put, I pray thee, thy hand under my thigh, and deal kindly and truly with me; bury me not, I pray thee, in Egypt: but I will lie with my fathers, and thou shalt carry me out of Egypt, and bury me in their burying-place. And he said, I will do as thou hast said." But this simple promise was not sufficient for the dying Patriarch; and he demanded of Joseph a still more solemn pledge, saying, "Swear unto me. And he sware unto him." The last words Jacob uttered were on this subject; for unto his sons assembled around his bed of death he said, "I am to be gathered unto my people: bury me with my fathers in the cave that is in the field of Ephron the Hittite, in the cave that is in the field of Machpelah, which is before Mamre, in the land of Canaan, which Abraham bought with the field of Ephron the Hittite for a possession of a burying-place. There they buried Abraham and Sarah his wife; there they buried Isaac and Rebekah his wife; and there I buried Leah." And they obeyed their father's dying charge; for they bore his lifeless body three hundred miles across the desert to the land of Canaan,—the servants of Pharaoh, the elders of the house of Joseph, and all the elders of the land of Egypt accompanying them: "there went up both chariots and horsemen; and it was a very great company." Joseph felt this strong natural instinct; and in his death took an oath of the children of Israel for his burial-place in Canaan, and "gave commandment concerning his bones." And that oath his descendants faithfully fulfilled. Amidst the plagues of Egypt, and the haste with which they came out from that land of bondage, they forgat not his body, but bore it with them to their first encampment, through the Red Sea, and through "that great and terrible wilderness," until they had crossed the Jordan, and had buried it in "Jacob's purchased possession," in the land of promise. Ruth, the Moabitess, felt it, and said to Naomi, her mother-in-law, when entreated to leave her, "Where thou diest will I die, and there will I be buried." We all feel this great natural instinct. We desire to sleep in companionship with our friends. Solitariness in burial is not what we desire. Who would not rather start up at the sound of the last trumpet amidst a family of the dead, than wake up alone in the empty wilderness? And who would not rather perish in a sea traversed by the ships of all nations, than sink, "unknelled, uncoffined, and unknown," in the midst of a mastless ocean? But especially do we desire to be buried with our kindred, —to sleep with our fathers. And although a necessary law, yet it is a severe law, which requires that for sanitary reasons the sacred freeholds of the dead, which have been purchased "for a possession of a burying-place," should be closed, and the dead of families should be divided. It shocks our natural instinct; it disturbs our cherished hopes of rest in the grave with our kindred. David, the man of sociable affections, had this desire for burial with the great and the good of his own people realized: "he was laid unto his fathers." This instinct was strong in that great servant of the Church whose decease brings us together to-night. He wished to be laid unto his fathers, in the best sense: that his body should be united with the bodies of the great Methodist labourers before him; and Providence so ordered it that in this strong natural craving he had his heart's desire.

We come to the closing passage of the text: "*And his flesh saw corruption.*" David's lot was the common lot of humanity. The principle of life,—we know not what it is in its essence,—that mysterious principle of life shall be withdrawn from the organized material frame; chemical laws which cannot act while that principle is present, shall commence their action,—the action of decomposition. The body shall become corrupt and putrid; the worm shall feed upon it and shall devour it. This is the penalty for sin that all must pay. Here "the rich and the poor meet together." This "one event happeneth unto all." "In Adam all die." "By one man sin entered into the world, and death by sin; and so death passed upon all men, for that all have sinned." Thus, "one generation passeth away, and another cometh." But, as we have seen concerning the servant of God and of his generation, "his flesh also shall rest in hope." They "who are fallen asleep in Christ" have not "perished;" but shall be "delivered from the bondage of corruption into the glorious liberty of the children of God."

How these great scriptural truths and lessons are sustained and illustrated in the life and services of him whose departure from earth has clothed us in mourning, and occasioned this sermon, I now proceed briefly to show.

SKETCH

OF THE

CHARACTER AND SERVICES

OF THE LATE

REV. JABEZ BUNTING, D.D.

It is a beautiful and impressive fact recorded for us in Holy Scripture, that, in primitive times, religious parents gave names to children significant of the circumstances of their birth, and which should render them living memorials of the special interposition of God on their behalf. Thus Hannah, the wife of Elkanah the Ephrathite, called the name of her late-born child Samuel, "because," said she, "I asked him of the Lord." And the name of Jabez was given to him whose memory we have now more especially to recal, with similar significancy of meaning.

After the Conference at Leeds, in the year 1769, Richard Boardman, Mr. Wesley's first Missionary to America, then on his way to embark for the New World, rode into the quiet and almost unknown village of Monyash, in Derbyshire, to rest for the night; and, as the custom was with the early Methodist itinerants, before retiring to sleep he preached to as many persons as could be hastily collected together. His text was taken from 1 Chron. iv. 9, 10: "And Jabez was more honourable than his brethren; and his mother called his name Jabez, saying, Because I bare him with sorrow. And Jabez called on the God of Israel, saying, O that Thou wouldest bless me indeed, and enlarge my coast, and that Thine hand might be with me, and that Thou wouldest keep me from evil, that it may not grieve me! And God granted him that which he requested." In that village congregation was an intelligent, thoughtful young woman, named Mary Redfern, who received the word gladly into her heart; and who, ten years afterwards, when she had married and settled in Manchester, gave to her first child, born on the 13th day of May, 1779, the name of Jabez, in grateful remembrance of the saving benefit she had received through the preaching of the travelling Missionary. Having spent some part of the time that elapsed between her conversion and her marriage with families in Manchester visited by Mr. Wesley, and having thus become personally known to him, she carried her babe to Oldham Street Chapel on the occasion of one of Mr. Wesley's pastoral visits to that town. Her purpose was, that the child might receive the benediction of the venerated founder of Methodism. And there Mr. Wesley took the infant Jabez Bunting into his arms, and solemnly blessed the child in the name of the Lord, and before all the congregation. Should we speak too strongly, if we were to say that the subsequent history of Methodism has shown that with that blessing was bequeathed Mr. Wesley's own mantle to that child?

Not much is known of Dr. Bunting's childhood. He has been heard to speak of the vivid remembrance he had of some of the Methodist Preachers whom he heard in his boyhood, and of the ineffaceable impression made upon his young mind by the placid and sweetly benignant countenance of the venerable Wesley. From his own testimony it would appear that, under God, he owed his first religious impressions to his mother; and, in common with that of numerous great men, the early formation of his entire character may also be traced to the maternal source. His father, William Bunting, a native of Monyash, was an intelligent, pious Methodist; but his mother's energetic and diligent devotion to the service of God most powerfully impressed him, and most decidedly influenced both his spirit and destiny. She prayed much for him and with him, instructed him in the great facts and principles of religion, watched over him with wakeful solicitude, took him with her to the house of worship, and trained him up for God's service. The firm and devoted character of his mother had been formed by struggle with difficulties and opposition. In early life she had endured persecution for the sake of Jesus Christ, and found the truth of the Scripture declaration, that foes shall be of our own household. She was born at Upper-Haddon, in Derbyshire, but subsequently removed with her parents to Monyash, where she heard Richard Boardman. Her father, instigated by the ungodly clergyman of the parish, with whom he was intimate, persecuted her for her attendance at Methodist services. And this he did so far at one time as to endanger her life, so that for personal safety she had to leave home and take a situation in Manchester. But a sense of duty to an afflicted mother brought her back to Monyash, where she had, to a great extent, the charge of her father's house, and where she was the means of imparting seasonable religious counsel to her almost helpless mother. She lived to see her son honourable and useful in the Church to which she had devoted him; died at a good old age in the house of her son-in-law, the Rev. Thomas Fletcher, who was at that time head-master of Woodhouse Grove School, near Leeds; and was buried beside her husband, in St. James's churchyard, Manchester.

His great obligation to her who thus brought him up in the nurture and admonition of the Lord he never forgot; and, to the end of his life, whenever he referred to his mother, it was with strong emotion. His boyhood seems to have been marked by outward purity, by the love of the Scriptures, and by delight in the public services of religion; and there were in his case, as in Timothy's, "prophecies (foretellings) that went before" of his future eminence in the Church of Christ.

By the blessing of Divine Providence upon their industry and frugality, his parents were able to provide for him a good education, and thus to prepare him for the important service he should afterwards render to the Church. They were enabled to place him, at a suitable age, in a large public school, where he was surrounded by the sons of many of the wealthier families of the town. Here he had to bear the reproach of Christ; for his haughty schoolfellows not only contemned him for his humbler birth, but on account of his Methodist parentage. This was felt so much at first, that, soon after his entrance into the school, his mother waited upon the master, and said that, unless the persecution of her son were abated, she must remove him. The master replied, he need not heed the persecution of the boys, for he would soon be at the head of the school. This prediction was speedily fulfilled; and, instead of being despised by his schoolfellows of wealthier parentage, he became the general favourite.

One of the scholars was the son of Dr. Percival, an eminent physician and man of letters in Manchester. This youth became ardently attached to young Jabez, introduced his accomplished schoolfellow into his father's family, and had the "head-scholar" there frequently as his companion during holidays. Dr. Percival was won by the superior intelligence and great amiability of this chosen companion of his son; and proposed to receive Jabez into his own house, as a student in the medical profession, and as his general assistant in literature. This proposal was acceded to by his parents, but with the expressed provision that their son should sleep under their own roof, and spend his Sabbaths wholly with them. This stipulation was the more carefully made, because Dr. Percival was not considered orthodox in his views as to the Divinity and Atonement of Christ. The intercourse of a youth of so much talent and excellence with a gentleman of refined literary taste, undoubtedly, did much to influence both his mind and manners, while the vigilant care of his mother prevented any evil effect that might have arisen from contact with heterodoxy. The daily association of the young Jabez with Dr. Percival, unquestionably, tended to give him that purity and finish in literary composition, and that gentlemanly courteousness of demeanour, which, in manhood, so eminently distinguished him. His proficiency in the medical profession was rapid and great; so that, within a comparatively short period, attractive and advantageous proposals for settlement in it were made to him by Dr. Percival; and the prospect of honourable and distinguished success in it opened before him.

But Jabez Bunting was designed by God for a higher service than that of the medical profession. He was fore-ordained to be a Minister of the Gospel of the Son of God, and to be a chosen vessel for spiritual service. His conversion was connected with an apparently trivial incident which, in its issues, had no small influence upon him as an administrator of discipline in the Church. From his childhood he had been accustomed to accompany his beloved mother to the lovefeasts of Methodism, as well as to its other special services. The Rev. Joseph Benson had been succeeded in Manchester by the Rev. Alexander Mather, a rigid disciplinarian, who gave positive orders that none but duly accredited members should be admitted to the lovefeasts; and that they, on their admission, should show their last quarterly tickets of membership. A lovefeast was to be held in Oldham Street Chapel; but Jabez Bunting, not being a member of Society, had to be left at home by his mother. "Jabez," said she to him, before she quitted him, "I do not know what you think of it; but to me it seems an awful fact that, after having been carried to the lovefeast when you were unable to walk, you should now be excluded from it by your own fault." Her words were as a nail fastened in a sure place: they pierced and fixed themselves within the very depths of his soul; and, in the loneliness of his situation, and in the poignancy of his grief, he went up into his bed-room, confessed his sinfulness, implored the Divine mercy, and very soon afterwards obtained, through faith in the blood of Christ, the divine assurance by the Spirit that his sins were all forgiven, and that he was the adopted child of God.

This fact, with other particulars of his early life, he related at the Centenary Meeting held in City Road Chapel, London; and they who were present at that memorable meeting will remember the emphasis with which he spoke, when, at the end of the relation, he said, "So that you see I have to thank God for Methodist discipline as well as for Methodist doctrine."

Immediately after his conversion, he joined himself to a weekly class, led by his uncle, Mr. Joseph Redfern. Mr. R. had followed his sister, the mother of Jabez, from Monyash to Manchester; and had there, principally through her instrumentality, been converted to God, and become a useful class-leader for the Oldham Street Society. Jabez Bunting's first ticket of full membership was received in the Christmas quarter of the year 1794; and it is remarkable that the text of Scripture which it bore was from Jabez's prayer: "O that Thou wouldest bless me indeed, and keep me from evil!" He had then passed into his sixteenth year; and a class-paper of that period, still extant, shows how regular the young disciple was in his attendance on that spiritual and quickening means of grace: for, in relation to his name, A, for "absent," is not once to be found on it. Thus Methodist discipline was practically observed by him, as well as associated in his mind with his conversion to God.

Having himself become a partaker of the saving grace of God, he became, under the constraining influence of the love of Christ, zealous and laborious for the salvation of others. He attended prayer-meetings that were held in private houses for the benefit of persons resident in their neighbourhoods, and took part in those exercises; and he went into the courts and alleys, and into the outskirts of the town, and sought, by earnest warnings and exhortations, to compel sinners to come in and be partakers with him of Gospel blessings. During this period he was most earnest in the endeavour to improve his own mind with scriptural and theological knowledge, and also to stimulate other minds around him to similar improvement. A Minute Book of a Young Men's Improvement Society, of which young Jabez Bunting was the secretary and the most active member, preserved by the son of an early Methodist in Manchester, bears, in its contents, full proof of this. His first public address is said to have been an open-air exhortation, which he delivered on a Sunday afternoon, in Salford; and his first sermon was preached in his nineteenth year, in a farm-house, at a place called Sodom, near to Blakeley, a few miles from Manchester. His text was, "Ye believe in God, believe also in Me;" and his most intimate friend, (the friend of his youth, as well as of his mature and declining life,) Mr. James Wood, of Grove House, Manchester, who was with him on the occasion, was wont to affirm that he never afterwards preached a better sermon than he did at Sodom on that day. His admiring friend may have been excited by a first performance, and have spoken from the overflowing warmth and partiality of friendship; but it is, nevertheless, true that early maturity was one of Dr. Bunting's most remarkable characteristics.

As might be anticipated, the call of the Church without, that he should separate himself from secular pursuits, and give himself wholly to the word of God and to prayer, was soon heard uniting with the divine call which he received in his own soul. That call he forthwith obeyed; and leaving all prospects of earthly advantage in Manchester, he went forth as a Methodist itinerant preacher,—one who should have no settled place of abode, and but a scanty, and in those days precarious, means for subsistence. The change of circumstances was felt the more by him, because it deprived him of the power of helping his widowed mother, (his father having died some two years previously,) as effectively as heretofore. Yet he did help her out of his very small income as a Methodist preacher; and he helped her as long as she lived. The Conference of 1799 gave him his first appointment: it was to the Oldham Circuit, when he was in his twentieth year. The incident he has been heard to describe, of his uncle Redfern accompanying him on the road from Manchester, as he went forth on foot towards Oldham, carrying his saddle-bags on his arm, and of their affectionate parting at a retired spot, where, before they separated, they prayed and wept together, must have been affecting indeed.

His preaching in the Oldham Circuit was with power; and the people greatly wondered at the wisdom with which he spoke to them. Mr. Bradburn was at that time stationed in Manchester; and the young preacher at Oldham—who, then as ever afterwards, was attracted by good speaking—used to visit his mother usually at the end of the week, and take the opportunity of hearing, on the Saturday evening, the prince of Methodist orators. Mr. Bradburn seems to have appreciated the superior talents of his young ministerial hearer, and to have received Jabez Bunting into free and intimate intercourse with himself; and deeply interesting and instructive were the reminiscences of Bradburn's sayings and doings which the friends of Dr. Bunting sometimes heard from him in free conversation.

The subsequent appointments of Dr. Bunting may be learned from the Minutes of Conference. From Oldham he removed to Macclesfield; and from thence he was appointed to London, when he was married in the Lord to Sarah, the pious and talented daughter of Mr. Maclardie, a professional and accomplished musician, who was organist at Christ's church (the Rev. David Simpson's) in Macclesfield, where Mr. Wesley sometimes preached. Then he was stationed in Manchester; and afterwards in Sheffield, Liverpool, Halifax, and Leeds, remaining in each Circuit two years, which was as long as the laws of the Connexion would at that period allow. He was then appointed again to Circuits in London, Manchester, and Liverpool, remaining in each Circuit three years, and serving, while in London, as senior secretary for the Missionary Society, and as editor for the Book Room. On the death of Richard Watson in 1833, he was re-appointed to be the senior secretary for the Missionary Society; and, for eighteen years afterwards, up to the Conference of 1851, he held that important office. He then retired from its full duties, and became a supernumerary; but, since then, at the special request of the Conference, from year to year, he gave the aid of his counsel to the missionary secretaries, and to the committee. From its establishment in 1834, to the end of his life, he was also president of the Theological Institution. During this extended period of fifty-nine years of ministerial service in Methodism, he faithfully devoted himself to the promotion of its interests. At an early part of his ministry he offered himself to be sent as one of Dr. Coke's first missionaries to India; but he was retained by his fathers and brethren for evangelical labour in his own country at home, they being loth to part with him for foreign service. This offering of himself for missionary service abroad he used to speak of with grateful satisfaction to the end of his days, being earnestly thankful for the grace which had led him to make it freely and unreservedly. "Some of the happiest moments of my life," he has been heard to say, "next to those that immediately followed my conversion to God, were when I fully presented myself to the Lord, as a missionary to India."

Soon after he was received into the ministry, Jabez was found more honourable than his brethren.

He rose rapidly into eminence, both as a preacher, and in the Conference; and though there were, in those days, several ministers of mark and of just celebrity in Methodism, yet he took full rank among them, and became an acknowledged leader in our Israel. By his effective and popular preaching he swayed the masses of the people; and by his business talent and statesmanlike dealing with subjects as they arose in the Conference, he gained ascendancy over the minds of his brethren; so that he soon became the most powerful man in Methodism. He was the first minister elected by nomination into the "Legal Hundred." When but a young man on trial, he aided Dr. Coke in the secretaryship of the Conference; he was the first to fill that office after the doctor's departure for India; and so efficiently did he perform its duties, that he was elected to it by his brethren not less than ten times. As many as four times, and those in years as near together as the regulations of the Body admit, he held the highest office that the Methodist ministry affords,—that of President of the Conference.

This high position he obtained, fairly and legitimately, by his commanding talents, and by his great and beneficial services to the Connexion. His energetic and comprehensive intellect grasped the real nature and genius of Methodism; and, seeing how its institutions required consolidation and expansion, he set himself to accomplish these objects, so as to adapt the whole machinery of Methodism more adequately to its advanced position and circumstances. And so great and extensive were his labours in these respects, and so fully did his prove to be the leading and master-mind of the Connexion, that during the last half-century there has scarcely been an important movement in Methodism that has not sprung, directly or indirectly, from him. Mr. Wesley, it is well known, organized Methodism in the shape of mere Societies, but refused to give it a complete and separate form of ecclesiastical government; and he left the pecuniary means for its support to be provided, in a great degree, as circumstances might require and favour, from time to time. Though this arrangement and procedure served very well during the life-time of the founder of Methodism, to whom all the numerous Societies were accustomed to look up with confidence and grateful veneration, yet immediately after his decease there were great anxieties and discussions on these matters, and several very important arrangements had to be made in relation to them. Still there remained much to be done to balance the system of Methodism, and to adjust it for safe and harmonious working. This service, under God, Dr. Bunting, with his surpassing qualifications of mind, most effectively supplied. He saw, for instance, that the nomination and election of the most senior ministers only into the legal hundred, and that wholly by the hundred themselves,—which, at first, was the rule,—would produce jealousy and discontent among the younger ministers, and thereby peril the unity of the Body; while the main responsibility for government must rest upon men who had passed the meridian of their strength. He therefore proposed and carried a plan for filling every fourth vacancy that should occur in the legal Conference with one younger minister, by nomination from all the members of the General Conference that have travelled fourteen years.

Again: he saw that the mode of aiding one fund in its necessity by taking from another which had been raised for a different purpose, was likely to produce discontent and complaint; and he drew up a scheme for the distinct and separate working of each fund of the Connexion, and for the yearly presentation of an account of the income and disbursements of each fund, distinctly and separately. He saw that the scattered laws and regulations of Methodism, which had accumulated in its progress, needed unity and relative agreement; and he set himself to accomplish this as occasion might arise, from time to time. His constant and persevering aim was to consolidate and complete Methodism as a system of evangelical agency; and to this work he devoted all the powers of his clear, constructive, and practical mind.

On the death of Dr. Coke, he became the chief

director of the Wesleyan Missionary movement, —the greatest Christian Missionary movement of any age. And to Jabez Bunting, more than to any other man, Wesleyan Missions owe their prominence and precedence among the great Protestant enterprises of Christendom. He was the chief agent in organizing the Wesleyan Missionary Society: he took the platform for its advocacy against the fears and doubts of many, and that with the most triumphant success. For many years, as we have seen, he served it as one of its general secretaries,—making for it one of the noblest sacrifices that a man possessed of such a mind could possibly make, in the considerate and resolute abandonment of long cherished literary projects. In a letter to a friend, written at the time when this resolve was made, he says, "The die is cast. If I give to our Missions the attention they require, I shall not have hereafter any time for literature." After the writing of that letter we have no more publications under the name of Jabez Bunting,—though there have been, since then, numerous important documents deposited in the archives of the Connexion that bear the unmistakeable impress of his powerful hand: so that his sermon on "Justification by Faith," preached before his brethren in the Halifax District,—his sermon preached before the Sunday School Union, in Dr. Winter's chapel, London,—and one or two memorials of departed Methodist labourers,—while they are sufficient to show us what the finished productions of his pen would have been, if his literary purposes had been carried out, yet they are all that he has left to perpetuate his name in connexion with literature; he having deliberately and determinedly sacrificed the thought of a literary career for practical service in the cause of God. But there is greatness in deeds, as well as in writing books; and the name of Jabez Bunting will be as illustrious through his labours for Missions and Methodist institutions, as if he had been the author of fifty folios. When stationed in Leeds, he had lucrative offers made to him by gentlemen belonging to the Society there, and who were desirous of having some of his powerful sermons published. They offered him, I believe, as much as £500 for the manuscripts of some twelve sermons. But he refused, on the ground of full occupation with his ministerial duties; and when urged to compliance by some of his intimate friends, on the plea of the probable requirements of his family, he replied, that if he were faithful in doing the work of his calling, God would provide for his family. He lived to see the fulfilment of his own saying; and to remark, in his latter days, that he saw it fulfilled.

He was the first to introduce laymen into the management of the missionary affairs of the Church, —and that against strong remonstrances from many of his elder brethren. From that beginning, he successfully urged the need and fitness of enlisting the service of laymen in every Connexional committee where financial business had to be transacted,—until it has become an acknowledged principle in British Methodism, that in all such cases laymen shall be associated in equal numbers with Ministers: the maxim of our fathers being now practically carried out: "Spiritual matters belong to the preachers, and temporal to the people." The regulations for securing the religious purity and efficient working of Sunday schools; the fund for the relief of embarrassed chapels; the Children's Fund; and the Auxiliary Fund, either originated with him, or were moulded anew under his counsel. The Theological Institution for the improvement of junior Preachers was his own creation; and he gave to it his fatherly counsel and attention, to the end of his life. The great Centenary movement, by which more than £200,000 were contributed by a grateful people for the several institutions of the Connexion, and by which the scale of contribution to the cause of God was so materially raised among us; as also the Relief and Extension Fund, by which £80,000 were obtained for the same objects,—were mainly projected and materially promoted by him. Indeed, there is not an institution or department of Methodism which does not bear, more or less, the stamp of his formative intellect. He has ploughed, so to speak, his own practical and harmonious character deeply into every part of the vast field of Methodism; and, more than any other man since Mr. Wesley, has framed and fashioned it as a system of evangelical and disciplinary agency; so that, instead of being, as it was, a mere Society, or adjunct of another Church, its elementary principles have been expanded and carried forth, until it is now well-nigh matured as a fully organized Church in itself. And yet, like Wesley, and other disinterested labourers for the Lord, he made no earthly gain for himself by what he achieved. He received only the ordinary income of a Methodist minister, which did not really supply his wants as a public man in Methodism; but which left him, in his necessities, to consume, to a considerable extent, the means that, in the progress of life, came to him by his family connexions, and which others would have stored up more carefully for old age, and for their children.

Thus, "his works praise him in the gate;" and he has signally exemplified, in himself and in his pre-eminent position, the sovereign precept of our Lord concerning greatness among His followers: "Whosoever will be great among you, let him be your minister; and whosoever will be chief among you, let him be your servant." He was great by service and practical usefulness. If a great man be one who does that which when done is of the highest importance,—or if real greatness be great power producing great effects,—then, assuredly, Dr. Jabez Bunting was a great man, and a prince in our Israel. He served the generation of his own people by the will of God.

Nor was the acknowledgment of his superiority confined to his own community. The leading men of the nation, and of other religious denominations, saw and acknowledged it. For many years he was publicly regarded as the representative man of Methodism, embodying in his declarations and conduct its principles and proceedings. Senators and legislators for the nation sought his counsel and service in the cause of humanity and in seasons of emergency. He was enthusiastically loyal to the throne and government of his country, and more than once braved—by public denunciations and remonstrances—furious revolutionists in disturbed manufacturing districts where he was stationed; but he as manfully resisted any proposed legislative encroachments upon the civil or religious rights of British subjects. He was an advocate for the emancipation of Roman Catholics from civil restrictions; but he was ever found ready to resist to the utmost Popish corruptions and intrusions. On the renewal of the East India Company's Charter some years ago, he strenuously sought to secure freedom for Christian and Missionary enterprises among the natives of India; and he was found not less zealous for this freedom at the close of his life. He was united with Wilberforce, Clarkson, Buxton, and Watson, in organized efforts for the freedom of the long-oppressed Negroes in the West Indies; he lifted up his voice unceasingly in Conference against the toleration of slavery by the Methodists of the Northern States of America, until the great separation of the Churches there on that question, in 1844; and he was foremost in proposals for friendly but faithful remonstrances with the brethren there, against their being partakers in any degree of the sin which Mr. Wesley fitly described as "an execrable sum of all villanies." From its commencement, he was the friend and earnest advocate of the British and Foreign Bible Society; and though, in remembrance of the scriptural declaration, that "the wisdom that is from above is first *pure,* then peaceable," he was careful not to commit himself to formal association with the Evangelical Alliance until the firm, scriptural, and Protestant basis of union was agreed upon, yet, when he found that he could "serve" in this "with a pure conscience," he gave himself heartily to it, became its senior honorary secretary, and continued to hold that office to the end of his days. Not to enumerate the strong and admiring testimonies given publicly to his character by leading men of the nation and the Church, it is worthy of remembrance that the venerable and good Dr. Chalmers, among the last entries of his diary, declared that he loved to the uttermost Dr. Bunting, "one of the best and wisest of men." Thus the recognition of Dr. Bunting's transcendent merit has not been confined to his own people, but has been found among all communities and classes of the nation. Indeed, through his zealous, persevering, and successful efforts for missionary and philanthropic objects, the "sound of him has gone out into the ends of the world."

"What were the main elements of a character so pre-eminently great and useful?" will be the natural inquiry. I shall not attempt any formal analysis of Dr. Bunting's character, but shall simply state what most distinctly impressed me during my observance of him in public and private life.

It was impossible to be with him, and to observe him closely, without being impressed with his *genuine simplicity*. He was guileless as a child in his plans and purposes. "Godly sincerity" underlaid and appeared in all he said and did. In this respect he was a "plain man." There were no folds in his character: no embroidered covering, to mislead another's mind and judgment: no crooked and concealed policy. He was open and straightforward in what he said and did; and this it was which secured for him such implicit confidence in the minds of all who really knew him. They saw and felt that he was to be most unreservedly trusted in all that he professed and undertook. This was seen by the friend and patron of his youth, Dr. Percival,—who so fully confided in his integrity as to make him a legal executor to his will. And this was shown, not only by his friends and supporters, but also by his opponents. Hence those who had been railing against him have been heard openly proposing, when under accusation by others, to leave the decision of their case wholly to him. Truthful and upright in himself, he was unsuspicious towards others, and that to an extent seldom found among men: thoroughly and unwaveringly honest himself, he was always ready to put the most favourable and kindly construction on the conduct of others,—even of his foes.

With this genuine and unaffected simplicity and unswerving uprightness, there were in him unaffected *humility* and real *kindness of disposition.* A more modest, self-forgetful man could scarcely be found. Conscious as he must have been of his own superior gifts, and of his power over others, there was no vaunting of himself on these accounts. From his mind boasting seemed to be entirely excluded. Even when in the freest intercourse with his most intimate friends, he seldom or ever referred to anything that he had done, though he had done so much; and nothing seemed to disturb him more than public references to his excellence or ability. And, thus truly and spiritually meek and lowly, he assumed no lofty airs of dignity or reserve. He did not screen himself off, by ceremonious stiffness, from his brethren in the ministry, and from the multitude, lest he should lose caste and *status* by too much familiarity with them. Some of my hearers will have remembrances of the Conference held at this town of Bradford in the autumn of 1853,—when, yonder in front of Kirkgate Chapel, numbers of

Methodist men and women, "loosened" at noon from the "mills," gathered to see the ministers leave the place of their assembly to go to the houses of friends who entertained them, and stretched forth their unwashed hands towards Dr. Bunting; and they will remember how hearty was his shake of fraternal recognition. He was a thoroughly kindly and courteous man: there was not, at any moment, anything approaching to moroseness or repulsiveness in his manners. He was not a gentleman in high places only: he was gentle and gracious in spirit, and therefore he was a gentleman always. Who ever knew him rude, or vulgar, in word or action? He might say, or do, what was strong and weighty in its pressure upon others who were contending against him; but never what was coarse or rude. He honoured woman, reverenced the aged, and loved little children. It were difficult to say whether his gentleness and attention to children, or the completeness with which he won their love at once, were the more remarkable. He was a hearty and companionable man. He loved the friendly circle, cheerfully joined in the evening hymn, joyfully listened to the sound of music, and was ever ready to prolong the fire-side conversation, rather than cut it short for early separation and retirement. Like Dr. Johnson, whom in some other respects he much resembled, he "liked to fold his legs and have his talk out."

In his home he was, as it is required of a Christian minister to be, "given to hospitality." Nothing appeared to please him more than to have a goodly number of his ministerial brethren around his table. And his friends throughout the kingdom will remember his cheerful and happy companionships with them in their several abodes after he had performed his public labours for the day; and how, though they viewed him as an oracle of wisdom, yet he sat among them and in the midst of their families, simple and open as a child. He was charmed by wit; for he had it, sharply and brightly, in himself: but he kept the dangerous weapon most guardedly under restraint. He knew well that indulgence in the habit of looking at things in a ludicrous light is hurtful to the moral feelings. Still, he loved to hear a cheerful sally of genuine humour, and would himself indulge, now and then, in a smart repartee. And whether at his own table, or at the friendly board of another, he would courteously listen to what might be related by any, of personal observations and experiences; and then, as one among the company, he would tell his own tale of bygone days and departed acquaintances; and, though always without lightness and trifling, yet not unfrequently he would relate his anecdote or story with almost youthful zest.

While, however, he was kind and generous to all, yet he did not undervalue the more private and confidential intercourse of social life. He knew the truth of Addison's statement, that "there is no such a thing as real conversation but between two persons." He loved a chosen friend, to whom, in free companionship, he could reveal the interior thoughts and feelings of his heart. And when once his friendship was fixed, it was found, ever afterwards, firm and immoveable. Throughout his life, he was never known to neglect or desert a friend. Steadfastness in friendship seemed to be his very oath of knighthood.

His affections for home and family were strong. He was a tenderly devoted husband; a loving father; and he was ever ready to embrace any opportunity that would bring all his family together, immediately around him. Birthday anniversaries, Christmas, and other festive seasons of the year, were sociably observed by him; and it was touching to see him in his old age, when confined to his chair at the fire-side, fondling upon his knees, or playfully endeavouring to interest, on the hearth-rug, the infant daughter of Mr. Joseph Bunting, his youngest son. In the time of family bereavement, while resolutely submissive under the stroke, yet he bowed himself down heavily in his sorrow, "as one that mourneth for his mother." The kindliness of his nature extended to dumb, irrational creatures, some of which were usually to be found either frisking in pleasure before him, or stretched for rest and warmth at his feet. He was no stoic, no ascetic,—no mere bust of human nature, all head and no heart. His large soul had large sympathies. He loved the great home of the world and of humankind.

But, with these artless, lowly, winning, and sociable qualities of his nature, there were, as already noted, *high intellectual endowments*. His perception was clear, rapid, and certain. He usually saw at a glance the full meaning and bearings of things. With him there seemed to be no confounding of things that differ; no mist, no confusion; but all was plain and open to his view. Hence, the readiness with which he could, in an emergency, stand forward to counsel or plead, in a case under consideration. Hence, the breadth and completeness of the view he took of any subject he discussed. And hence, the clear and accurate forms of expression with which he instantly presented his views to the minds of others. He was undoubtedly endowed with marvellous power and facility of speech, so that he could give the most exact and ready enunciation of his thoughts at any time; but the pellucid clearness and cogent strength of his style proved the clearness and strength of his mental perceptions. Speech is but the outward and audible embodiment of the inward operations of thought; and if the one be weak, confused, and hazy, the other may be expected to be equally inane, chaotic, and nebulous. Style is but the image of the mind; and, in this respect, as in others, "As a man thinketh in his heart, so is he." Dr. Bunting's style of language was most simple and familiar: so much so, that it was no uncommon thing for persons who heard him speak, to affirm that they thought it would be very easy to say what he was saying, and in the very same form and order of words. But such a clear and complete style of speaking as his, is, in reality, the most difficult to attain, and therefore is very seldom found. It does not admit of a random or chance-medley use of words; but requires that the right words, and the right words only, should be employed, and that they all should be put in their right places. It is easy to affect a swollen, pompous style, and to use words twice as large as the subject needs; but it is not so easy, in the process of extemporaneous speaking, to pitch at once upon the fittest words, and to arrange them in their proper connexions. It requires clearness and precision of thought for this, as well as accurate and extensive knowledge of language. Dr. Bunting's style of speaking was so remarkably clear and complete, that what he said seemed fit at once for the press. Sometimes there was the use of long sentences, and of parenthesis,—the expanded and guarded reflection of a mind of "large discourse, looking before and after;" but who ever heard him speak obscurely or confusedly? or who ever thought, as they listened to him, that better words could have been employed to express the meaning?

With clearness and rapidity of view, he was logically precise and exact in his process of reasoning. Some persons have ready perception and great volubility of speech; but they reason incorrectly, and pronounce wrong conclusions. It was not so with Dr. Bunting. He pursued questions fairly from their acknowledged premises to their true and legitimate issues. He advanced from position to position, glancing at all sides of his subject as he passed onwards, until, by the time he had finished speaking, the argument he had constructed seemed as clear, as firm, and as harmonious as the architecture of the heavens. It has been said that he was utterly devoid of "genius" and "imagination." Well: it is true that he built no castles in the air, he spun no metaphysical cobwebs, he never soared into the heavens on the silken wings of prurient fancy. He seldom quoted poetry, except from the Methodist Hymn Book, Dr. Young's "Night Thoughts," George Herbert's "Temple," or some poem of ancient date. He based all he said and did on the solid ground of facts. But if "genius" be shown in the doing of something with surpassing excellence, and if "imagination" be that leading and commanding faculty of the mind that goes before to pioneer the course of thought, and that marshals the forces of argument, then it would be a vain task for any one to attempt to show that Dr. Bunting was devoid of genius and imagination. Facility in reasoning was, with him, as marked as facility of speech. He might be said to walk surely, in arguing: he did not stumble, or amble in his course: he did not "jump to a conclusion;" but pursued his way steadily until the true end was gained. For this cause he almost uniformly took the greater number of the minds he addressed along with him, in his pleadings; and made them wonder how it was, that they had not before seen the matter under consideration in the light in which he had placed it. Even when the subject under discussion had become complicated and entangled by the multiplied and conflicting opinions of others, he would seize the clue and unravel the whole with apparent ease. As Dr. Leifchild said at his burial, when referring to his practical counsel on difficult matters in early meetings of the Evangelical Alliance, "The wisdom of his suggestions, his counsel, and his advice, was soon perceived and felt; and ever after, when he rose, all was hushed to silence. Often, when we found ourselves involved in perplexity upon some topic before us, the sound of his voice was heard, and came like light upon the thicket, showing us the way out, and leading us to the proper result. In the extent of his information, the comprehensiveness of his views, the conclusiveness of his reasoning, and, I will add, in the urbanity of his manner, I never saw his equal, and I never expect to do."

Hence, as it might be expected, he was a man of sound and confident judgment. His conclusions, like his reasonings, were clear and certain; so that nearly all persons who heard him concurred with him in them. This fact was the basis of their attempted defamation on the part of those who envied him. They set him forth as wielding despotic power over his brethren, and as lording it over the wills and opinions of the members of Conference. But this was most flagrantly untrue. The minds he swayed were accustomed to weigh deliberately what was brought before them, and not listlessly and helplessly to lean upon others for their decisions. Finding him so uniformly just and sure, they could not but respect his judgment, and be disposed to hearken to him; but it was by fair and legitimate reasoning he brought them to approve the conclusions he affirmed.

In a word, he was a man of *influence and power*. And this was felt wherever he appeared. As Johnson said of Burke,—if you had met him accidentally under a gateway in a shower of rain, you would have known that he was a great man. In bodily figure and form he was a noticeable personage. View him where you might,—in the street, by the fire-side, on the platform, in the pulpit, or in a Committee,—his outward appearance, like his mind, was simple and impressive. If seated among a thousand men in a public assembly, a stranger among the spectators would be sure to inquire concerning him: "Who is that venerable-looking minister, with the large bald compact head, and with the plain single-breasted coat?" Tall, broad, massive, and upright in figure, and open in countenance, he was conspicuous even in a crowd; while his simple, devout, and thoughtful demeanour produced an immediate impression that he was no ordinary man. But it was the real superiority of his character which made him powerful. It was this which, in all the combinations of its excellence, drew others towards him, and cemented their attachment to him. Events follow the true hero. A superior mind will influence inferior minds as surely as the moon heaps up the waves of the Atlantic in her track. "What means did you employ?" was the question eagerly asked of one who had surprisingly succeeded in winning over to her cause Mary de Medici; and the simple answer was, "Only that influence which a strong mind has over a weaker one." It was so with Dr. Bunting, and the influence he exerted over others: the greater mind led and swayed lesser minds. Some complained of this; but they might, as rationally, have complained of the magnetic attraction of the North Pole: the laws of mind are as irresistible as the laws of matter. When Dr. Bunting first associated himself with the Evangelical Alliance, some were jealous of his apprehended power, having heard of his sway in the Methodist Conference; and they expressed their jealousy by saying, earnestly, "But he is not going to govern us!" The same parties were afterwards heard to say, "What a wonderful man is this Dr. Bunting of Methodism! He governs and sways us, as if we were children around him!" "He was born to rule," as Dr. Leifchild said; "but," as the same speaker added, "his rule was not that of assumed authority: it was the necessary and natural effect of a superior mind upon other minds, and which could not but determine their course." There are kings in the realm of mind as well as among nations; and Dr. Bunting was one of them. Yet, in his case, there was no effort to make an impression; to win favour or admiration. There was no bustle or show in what he did. He despised noisy popularity, and never courted it. A serene atmosphere, for the most part, surrounded him; and a calm and dignified demeanour, a real majesty of character, inspired respect and veneration towards him from all around. In him it was seen how commanding worth sits crowned in all companies.

These high gifts and powers he devoutly consecrated to the service of God. In his youth he had solemnly vowed himself to the Lord; and his faithful heart never drew back from the covenant. He gave all to his Divine Saviour, and kept back no part of the promised offering. He was a truly devout, spiritual, and prayerful man. There was, in all that he did, that deep tone of piety which nothing but frequent communings with God can secure. As Richard Watson said of him to a young friend, (young at that time,) the Rev. John Scott, "He was a great man, and did everything in the fear of the Lord." He laid hold on God's strength for what he had to do. He prayed to his Father who seeth in secret, and he was rewarded openly. He loved *social prayer*; and at the end of each petition by a friend he would fervently breathe his emphatic "Amen!" Some of my own most hallowed recollections of Dr. Bunting are connected with social prayer, when we addressed, alternately, the throne of grace. And those who heard him in public prayer can never forget him. Such reverence, such profound prostration of the soul, such enlargement of desire and fulness of petition, such pleading and continuance before the mercy-seat, such rising into confidence and holy boldness, and then such thrilling awe and overwhelming power, when God bowed the heavens and came down! These blessed remembrances must ever remain with those who heard his petitions to heaven on public occasions. He had, with his other gifts, pre-eminently, the gift of prayer; and he diligently cultivated and improved it. He seemed ever to live and to act in the spirit of dependence upon God; and, undoubtedly, this was the great source of his strength.

As a *Preacher*, he was lucid, orderly, and powerful. His chosen motto would seem to have been, "Commending ourselves to every man's conscience in the sight of God." He was natural and easy in his style, richly evangelical in his doctrine, and irresistibly impressive in his applications. He was not a startling preacher, after the manner of modern times. He glided easily into his subject, usually pointing out the position and connexion of the text in his introduction; and then, having clearly and fully explained the truth under distinct heads, he applied it with cogent appeals to the heart and conscience. There were no grotesque or incongruous views expressed to produce amazement or arrest attention; no spasmodic sentences,—the sure evidence of dislocated and ungoverned thought; no Germanizing of the English language, in order to give the appearance of originality to what was spoken; no essayizing of the form of the sermon, by the omission of *First, Secondly,* and *Thirdly;* and no toning down of Scripture terms for sin, wrath, and hell, to accommodate polite ears. He did not attempt to elaborate and adorn the truth until it was hidden and smothered by words of man's wisdom. He did not hang upon the Cross garlands of human oratory, or cover it with the tinsel ornaments of tropes and figures. He did not mince into feebleness the threatenings and commandments of the Divine Law. Sinai was a mount trodden by him, as well as Calvary; and thunderings and lightnings in his preaching, as in the Divine manifestations, preceded the proclamations of Almighty goodness and mercy. The "terrors of the Lord" he employed for the conviction of sin; and then the declarations of the Gospel for the healing of wounded souls. He not unfrequently set forth stern, legal views of Divine truth in his preaching; but Christ, as a just God and a Saviour, was ever proclaimed faithfully and fully. The atonement and the priesthood of Christ; the glory and extent of His dominion; the gift of the Holy Spirit; and the fulness of all spiritual blessings for the believer, were themes on which he delighted to dwell and to expatiate. St. Paul's Epistle to the Romans, which first concludes all under sin, and then declares God's righteous method of justifying them that believe in His Son, was his favourite section of the word of life. The eighth chapter of that Epistle, which, in one of his sermons, he described as being "a catalogue, or inventory, of the believer's privileges," was exceedingly precious to him. He had, as we have seen, a discriminating intellect; and this was evident in the pulpit as elsewhere. Sharp, fine distinctions characterized all his speaking. Sometimes, when preaching, he would open out a common and familiar word in a text of Scripture, so as to surprise and charm his hearers; but he never frittered down a passage into loose and unconnected morsels by verbal criticism. He knew how, with a fair and full exposition, to preserve the breadth and entirety of truth. And that truth he preached: he proclaimed and published it as a herald, and as an ambassador for God. He did not argue and debate upon it, as if it were of doubtful authority. He did not consult men's taste: he commanded it; and, after the manner of his Master, he spake as "one having authority."

His sermons were carefully prepared and digested before he delivered them. He brought no unbeaten oil into the sanctuary; and, while entirely dependent upon God for unction and success, yet he did not trust the composition of his discourses to happy frames and impulses: he did not unreasonably look for the ability to do suddenly in the pulpit what he could not do so well prayerfully and deliberately in his study. He practically received the statement, that "God's help begins where natural means can go no further; and that as far as these means are available, we are not warranted to expect extraordinary help." His mind seemed to be imbued with theology; and, like his other possessions of knowledge, this was systematized and full-orbed within him. He knew of what he spake; and having carefully prepared for the delivery of Divine truth, he was not afraid to reiterate it. He avowedly preached the same sermons in different places, knowing that he had the examples of Christ and His Apostles to justify him in so doing. Yet, he was no slave to pulpit preparations. His preaching was from the full devotion of his soul, and not merely from his memory; and, therefore, he left himself free for enlargement under the leadings of the Holy Spirit. And sometimes, like St. Paul, he was ready to preach until midnight. He had no more idea of preaching short, set sermons, which should just come within the measured three-fourths of an hour, and by no means exceed that prescribed limit, than had John Howe, or Richard Baxter,—two of his favourite authors in practical theology. Execution was his aim; and, therefore, he was unwilling to cease until he had done what he could to accomplish his object. Indeed, a "full service" might always be anticipated where he was to officiate. He loved the Methodist Hymn Book, and gave out its verses with the most appropriate tones and emphasis. He often quoted from it most aptly in his sermons; and threw, from its rich treasury of Christian doctrine and experience, helpful light upon the truth he was setting forth. He devoutly rejoiced in the use of the liturgy of the Church of England during Sabbath-morning service; and he never abridged the Scripture lessons to make room for his own sermon. As a minister of the sanctuary, he did all things reverentially, so that sometimes the public services he conducted were long; but they were so impressive and spiritual that few, if any, who attended them wished them to be shorter.

From the frequent mention he made of the Rev. Joseph Benson, and from the admiring description he was wont to give of that excellent man, as a preacher, it might almost be inferred that he was thus setting before us his model. But Dr. Bunting's preaching was less critical and expository than Mr. Benson's, while it was equally piercing and powerful in application. He was, in his preaching, no slavish imitator of any one: more than most men he was his own model, and in this respect called no man "Rabbi."

The effect of his preaching was exceedingly powerful. The unction of the Holy Spirit attended it, and rendered it signally successful in awakening and saving the souls of his hearers. I have heard statements concerning the striking results of his ministry, from aged Methodists in Leeds, Manchester, and London, that exceeded all I have heard of almost any other Methodist preacher. There were seasons of grace and salvation under his preaching, when large numbers together were cut to the heart, and cried out, "Men and brethren, what shall we do?" One such season in Grosvenor Street Chapel, Manchester, will never be forgotten. His manner, ordinarily, was not boisterous; but chastened, and fully under his control. There was, usually, a serene air about him,—a peaceful reverence in his look and demeanour,—when in the pulpit, that seemed fully in accordance with a Sabbath service, and which compelled the calm and serious attention of an assembly to what he said. His voice was clear and full, and capable of great variety of modulation. His action was as simple as it could well be. The left hand usually held the nearest corner of the Bible; and the right hand was slightly elevated towards the breast, and partially open, or otherwise spread horizontally over the page. His whole manner was calmly confident and collected. But, when roused to full energy under the power of the Holy Spirit, as was not unfrequently the case toward the end of his sermons, his face would become highly flushed, and his personal emotion so strong, that his friends feared the effects upon his life. On such occasions he would seize the sinner's conscience, and hold it with a firm grasp, while he threatened, reasoned, and expostulated; and then close upon the sinner, with beseeching and overwhelming earnestness, to repent and look to Christ for salvation. Dr. Leifchild, in the funeral address already quoted, expressed the judgment of many, besides his own, when he said, "I never heard such preaching before, and I have never heard such preaching since." The pulpit was really the throne from which this prince of preachers wielded such surpassing influence among men; and no minister of Christ can rule well in the Church who does not, first, compel the homage of the people by an effective ministry in the pulpit.

Great a preacher, however, as he was himself, he despised no one who, "according to the wisdom given unto him," preached Christ the all-sufficient Saviour of sinners. The youngest and most unlearned preacher of the Gospel, if simple and earnest, would find in him a ready counsellor and friend. Ardent, laborious zeal in the cause of God, by whomsoever manifested, had his cheerful commendation. The Rev. John Smith, whose burning zeal for the salvation of men consumed him at an early age, had Dr. Bunting's declaration of fraternal admiration and regard when men of lesser minds were doubtful as to the propriety of the plans of that true Revivalist. Indeed, reverence and love for the ministerial character was a prominent trait in him: he regarded it as sacred, and was careful never to depreciate or degrade it by any means whatever. And perhaps no presbyter of the Church of Christ ever did more to elevate and maintain it by his demeanour than he did. He loved all his brethren in the ministry, sympathized with them in their toils, wept with them in their sorrows, rejoiced with them in their triumphs, and was most tenderly and scrupulously careful of their reputation and credit. He lived, as it were, in the whole Methodist Connexion at home and abroad, and that from day to day: so that whatever affected his brethren affected him; and perhaps no man since the apostolic age could have used the words of St. Paul more comprehensively than he: "And beside what comes upon me daily, the care of all the Churches." He was one of the best hearers of a sermon that a preacher could possibly have: if the aim to do good was evident, the preacher would be sure to have from him an expression of approval. I have spent many a long Sabbath evening with him, towards the end of his life, when he was not able to preach twice a day himself, and have heard his opinion of preachers without number; and, with one solitary exception,—when a young candidate for the ministry had preached about the stars, before him,—I do not remember a word of disapproval, or of depreciatory criticism upon any sermon he had heard. He had always some good things to say of the preacher, and none that were evil. He was no detractor from the merits of his brethren; and was utterly free from the mean envy which grudges words of praise for others, and claims all for self. He was a generous, noble, magnanimous servant of the Lord, seeing and acknowledging variety and usefulness in all God's works and instruments, and rejoicing to see able and successful labourers springing forth and increasing around him.

As a Minister put in charge with circuits at home, and afterwards as a secretary intrusted with the oversight of Missionaries and their infant Churches abroad, he was able and faithful. His holy soul shrunk from sin; and therefore he would not tolerate it anywhere. Yet, if there were signs of genuine repentance in any who had fallen, he was ready to restore them in the spirit of meekness. His veneration for the aged, and his love for the young, were alike remarkable. He breasted a tide of tumultuous opposition to secure the exclusion of secular instruction from Sabbath schools, and sought to have the lambs of the flock "fed after their manner." Few ministers in Methodism have baptized more infants than he; and many parents and members of congregations will long remember the earnest, impressive addresses he delivered to them on the administration of that sacrament. He was a scriptural bishop, who took care of the whole flock over which God had made him overseer; and his written thoughts on pastoral duties, contained in what are called the "Liverpool Minutes,"—in his "Instructions to Missionaries,"—as well as in his Presidential charges to newly received Ministers, show how deep, comprehensive, and earnest, were his views and feelings in relation to the office of a Christian shepherd.

Any sketch of Dr. Bunting would be incomplete and disappointing, if it did not make reference to his *practical business talent*, and especially to his *surpassing power in debate.* Like all first-class minds, his was variously great. It was impossible to see him engaged in any manner without perceiving his superiority. Indeed, it was the harmonious combination of so many high qualities in him that gave him such decided pre-eminence; so that they who observed him carefully were often heard to say that, with his various talents, he must have been great in anything he had undertaken. His was a thoroughly practical English mind: he could not squander existence in Coleridgean dreaminess and useless speculation; he must be active in himself, and see the realization of his plans, in order to be happy. But his ready and mighty intelligence was most apparent in debate, and especially in reply; and they who never heard him in public discussion on an important subject cannot estimate aright his transcendent ability. In Committee and in Conference ordinarily he was chary of his remarks. He sought, now and then, by a few words, gently to guide the opinions of others, rather than to control and govern them,—thus giving others to feel, as much as possible, that they were really performing the work to be done, rather than doing it under his direction; and knowing that frequent and unimportant speeches are regarded by men of business as vexatious, and that the uttering of them would surely result in a loss of influence. And if he spoke for more than five minutes, it would be when nearly all had spoken who were disposed to speak, and that to harmonize the discordant opinions, allay any perturbation of feeling, or to settle at once the question under consideration. But if any important measure were strenuously opposed, then the giant was roused to put forth all his might, and he came forth upon the opponents with tremendous force. While the adverse speeches were being made, he would sit and listen most attentively,—bowing his head forward, now and then,—and, perhaps, enclosing his ear in his hand, that he might be sure to hear all that was spoken; and, if he took any notes at all, they would be the merest jottings on the back of a letter with a pocket-pencil. Then, when all others taking part in the discussion had spoken, he would rise, and answer all that had been said, in the most orderly and complete manner possible. As it appeared to others, if he had been allowed weeks for the review of what had been advanced, and for preparing his answer, the reply could not have been given more satisfactorily and fully than when it was given thus instantly and extemporaneously.

He usually commenced his reply by guarding the subject under consideration, and his views concerning it, from misunderstanding and abuse. He then accepted what had been said by any preceding speakers, so far as it would strengthen his own position; and, not unfrequently, he would speak in complimentary terms of the spirit and manner which the opponents had displayed in stating their objections. But after this, and after giving reasons for the view he himself held, he would not unfrequently come down upon both the speakers and their arguments with crushing power, so that you wondered how those who were receiving such heavy and fast-falling blows could survive them; and you perceived that all felt they could breathe more freely when they had heard all he was disposed to say concerning themselves, and what they had been advancing. If any great essential principle of Methodism had been assailed or brought into question, or if anything had been proposed that savoured of selfishness, he would be sure to strike hard and heavy blows; and some words of sharp rebuke would be spoken that would long be remembered. Whoever touched any of the essential elements of Methodism touched the very apple of his eye; and in the protection of Methodism, and its defence, he spared neither friends nor foes: the conservation and welfare of the cause of Christ was dearer to him than any friends; and this was manifest in all he said and did. When roused, he was bold and courageous as a lion, for truth and righteousness: the most formidable and threatening opposition would not make him quail; and, like Luther, he would have breasted confederated hosts.

But while thus resolutely conservative of great and essential principles in Methodism, he was, from the beginning of his public life, as we have seen, an earnest and persevering advocate for its progress and development. As one has said, "It is a fact but little known, and, by those who have been accustomed to hear this great man railed at as a priestly dictator, not even suspected, that nearly every measure which has popularized the institutions of Methodism, and which has given to the people a more liberal representation, has originated with Dr. Bunting." He led the way in all plans for the real advancement of Methodism, keeping it safe from the furious rush of democracy on the one hand, and the corrupting tendencies of high ecclesiasticism on the other; and he was never satisfied with its working, either at home or abroad, if it did not make distinct and positive inroad upon the dominion of Satan and the world.

And though so devoted and attached a Methodist, yet his heart was large and catholic in its sympathies towards all the various sections of the Church of Christ. He venerated the Church of England as the mother Church of Methodism; he praised Nonconformists for their conscientious resistance of oppression, and for their persevering struggles for liberty to serve God; he sympathized with the Free Church of Scotland in its struggle for spiritual freedom, and aided it in its endeavours to cast off the yoke of secular authority. He loved all of every name that called upon the Lord Jesus Christ for salvation; and he was ready to associate with them in plans of philanthropy and benevolence, so far as circumstances would allow. He loved the name of "Christian" more than the name of "Methodist;" and was too large-hearted to suppose that pure and undefiled religion was only to be found within the pale of his own Church.

It was too much to expect that one so preeminently great and good should escape reproach and persecution; but he proved himself able, through Divine grace, to suffer for Christ, as well as to speak and to labour for Him. Perhaps no distinguished member of the Church of God in modern times has been more violently assailed, or more grossly misrepresented, in his character, plans, and motives, than Jabez Bunting; and yet he was not careful to answer what was said or written against him. He had the unquailing boldness and fortitude of a martyr for the cause of Christ; but his own reputation he nobly left to uphold and support itself as it might. Between others and himself personally he left God to defend the right. If Shimei cursed him, he let his enemy curse on; and still pursued his own course of Christian labour. He lived down calumny and reproach by a holy and unblameable life of consistent goodness; and he was spared to see the Jerusalem that he loved become a peaceful and a prosperous habitation. And if he be the strongest man who can bear the heaviest weight without staggering, then, in this view also, Dr. Bunting was strong and great.

In the earlier part of his ministry, he was thin and somewhat weak in his bodily frame; and there were times when both he and his friends feared that his life would be prematurely cut short by his earnest labours. He was a hard student, and sometimes drew largely upon the night for reading, thought, and pulpit preparation. His connexional services were incessant, and his efforts in preaching greatly exhausted him. But his strength increased as he advanced to maturity; and though in the latter period of his life he was seldom free from bodily weakness or pain, yet his continuance upon earth, until his eightieth year, proves that his physical constitution was, on the whole, sound and good.

At the Conference of 1849, he retired from the full duties of his office, and became a supernumerary. But, after this, his presence, counsel, and advocacy were sought, and found to be most valuable, in the several departments of Methodism.

As long as his bodily strength would allow him to attend, and to exercise his rare and precious gifts, he was seen in the Annual Conference of his brethren; and in the numerous Committee meetings in London; as well as in the pulpit and on the platform. To the end of his days his strong and vigorous understanding did not forsake him: he used to complain repeatedly to his friends, that his memory failed him, and that he was not able, as aforetime, to think connectedly; but there was little evidence of this to them. His remembrance of minute and particular circumstances, of persons and things, was, as ever, marvellous; and he could still take clear and comprehensive views of measures, though it was, of course, with greater effort, and it was followed by greater exhaustion. Methodist friends in London will remember that when, as he was pleased to say, he was no longer able to "make a speech," he took the chair at their several missionary meetings, and graced the platform by his venerable figure. His last missionary sermon—preached in the Centenary Hall, Bishopsgate, in

April, 1852, and which he read for a while, until he broke away from the manuscript, and poured forth his heart and mind in extempore sentences—will never be forgotten by Methodists of the present generation who heard him. And that scene in Exeter Hall, when, on his last appearance on our missionary platform there, in May, 1857, the whole multitude at the annual meeting rose *en masse*, spontaneously, to greet him, as he stood up to speak, will never be effaced from any mind upon which it was then imprinted. His interest in the work of God remained to the end of his life unabated; and, as far as he had strength, he gave it for the promotion of the cause of his Redeemer.

On reaching the age of threescore and ten, he evidently realized the shortening of his days; and he spoke seriously to his family and friends of his arrival at the assigned limit of human life. At the death of Robert Newton, his friend and contemporary in the ministry, he spoke still more earnestly on this subject; and those who knew him intimately, and observed him closely, will remember a period when he began to utter every word and perform every act, as it were, with eternity immediately before him. A sleepless guard seemed placed over his every step; and he lived with the constant remembrance that he might die at any moment. During the last two or three years, bodily infirmities had so increased upon him that he could take little share in any public duties. And, though he loved life and enjoyed it, he was willing to sink back into retirement and see others perform the services which had formerly devolved upon himself. He was cheerfully contented with his lot; and said that he had had his own day of service, and must now leave active employment to others.

His last sermon was preached for me, at Brixton, in the Lambeth Circuit, on Sunday Morning, September the 3rd, 1854, from the ninth verse of the first chapter in the First Epistle of St. John: "If we confess our sins, He is faithful and just to forgive us our sins, and to cleanse us from all unrighteousness;" and it was accompanied with special unction from above. Like the beloved Apostle when he wrote the text, the preacher of that morning was full of years and full of grace; and he spoke as a loving father to his children on the faithfulness and justice of God, in pardoning and purifying the guilty and polluted souls of penitent, believing sinners. Before he commenced his sermon, he was timid with the apprehension that he would not be able to proceed with it; for, on the previous occasion of his attempting to preach, (which was at Loughborough, in Leicestershire,) he lost the power of audible speech before he reached the end of his discourse. But, at Brixton, his voice was good, and his articulation clear and distinct; and he afterwards rejoiced in the remembrance that he had, once more, preached Christ. He had often said that preaching was his most delightful work, and so he found it in his last sermon. His last public ministerial service was that of baptizing the infant child of Professor Williamson, (the grand-child of his friend, the late Rev. Robert Wood,) in Oxford Road Chapel, Manchester.

Previous to the Conference of 1857, when laden

with domestic sorrow, I visited him for his fatherly sympathy and counsel. I found him manifestly more feeble and infirm than when I had seen him a few weeks before. He was confined to his "study," and was reclining on a sofa near the fire-place. We conversed, prayed, and wept together; and when I left him to return home, and received from him a token of paternal affection, "sorrowing most of all for the words he spake," that we might not meet again on earth, it was with the memorable words of David for Jonathan, passing and repassing through my mind: "Very pleasant hast thou been to me: thy love to me was wonderful; passing the love of women." He was not able to attend the Conference in Liverpool, but sent from his home in Myddelton Square, London, an affectionate message to his assembled brethren, by his friend and neighbour, Dr. Hoole,—assuring them that he should die in the faith of evangelical Arminianism; that his attachment to Methodism, its doctrines and discipline, was thorough and unabated; and requesting their prayers to God for him, that he might have a peaceful end. A letter was sent to him from the Conference, expressing the prayerful sympathy and reverential love of the brethren towards him; and his heart was filled with grateful pleasure by the reading of it. After this, he visited Buxton, Bath, and Manchester, and obtained partial relief; but he now abandoned all hope of again taking a part in public exercises, and said—*his work was done.* On his return, he was confined to his house, being unable any more to attend public worship. But, in his arm-chair by the fire-side, he was still the same sociable, cheerful, and companionable husband, father, and friend; he still showed unabated interest in the cause of God; and, as readily as ever, gave his counsel to those that waited upon him for it. After this, he suffered severely from influenza; and for the last seven months of his life was confined to his bedroom. In the day-time, he sat in an easy chair at the foot of the bed, partially leaning on the bed for support, and nursing his arm, which continuously suffered acute pain. I saw him in that state in February last, when I slept at his house, and had long conversations with him on the state and prospects of the Connexion, and on his own spiritual experience. He rejoiced greatly at the good news reported to him of the conversion of sinners, and exclaimed fervently as he heard it, "Praise the Lord!" He expressed deep concern for the rising ministry among us, that it should be preserved—amidst the errors and extravagancies of the times—evangelical and soul-saving in its character. He spoke on the great importance to Methodism of the proper training of candidates for its ministry at the Theological Institution, and of his own grateful feeling for the devoted and faithful labours in its two branches by its Tutors and Officers. He also spoke at length upon the importance of our people maintaining family religion and worship; and related how, in the days of Butterworth, Bulmer, and others whom he named, Methodist parents, in their social and neighbourly visits, would, if remaining to supper, leave the company for a time in the evening, go to their own homes for family worship, and then return to sup with their friends.

Now, towards the end of life, as aforetime, he was not anxious concerning the "Methodism of the future," nor disposed to foretel what it would be. His principle through life had been, to perform present duty, and leave events with God. It was so still: he committed Methodism and its interests unreservedly to the Divine keeping, and left all confidently there. And it was so with himself: referring to his own weak and afflicted condition, he said, with a peaceful smile which spread its radiance over his fine, fatherly countenance, "I am in the hands of the Lord, and am waiting till my change come!" He declared his only trust to be in the all-sufficient atonement of Christ, and affirmed, emphatically, "I have peace!" Indeed, it was impossible to be with him in his last affliction, and not see how harmoniously his Christian graces were adjusting themselves in the furnace, and how fully patience was having, in him, her perfect work. There was entire resignation to the Divine will for longer continuance on earth, while there were also meek and longing looks cast at times towards the heavenly land.

And none who visited him in his chamber, and beheld him leaning, with pain in his arm, on the chair or the end of the bed,—and with his comely face bordered by the black velvet cap which he wore in his latter days,—could fail to be deeply impressed with that picture of patriarchal submissiveness.

At his own request, I invited Bishop Simpson, from America, who had expressed a wish to see him, to visit him that day. At the interview which followed, he inquired with deep interest into the state of religion and of Methodism on the American continent; spoke of what he had seen of Dr. Coke, the first Methodist bishop there; related the conversion of his mother, through the preaching of Richard Boardman; and how he himself bore the name of Jabez, from the text taken at Monyash. He then had brought up to him, in his bed-room, for the bishop to see, Mr. Boardman's own staff, which the itinerant Missionary had used in journeying over America, and sent as a dying bequest to the doctor, and in token of affectionate regard.

I saw Dr. Bunting again at the beginning of May last, just after he had had an alarming bleeding in the mouth. He looked pale and wasted, and was suffering excruciating pain in his left arm; but there was still the same peaceful smile upon his countenance; and, as I approached him, he said, "I am glad to see you once more, for I am near the end of my days." Increasing weakness, as well as pain, was pressing him down to death, so that he could say but little of anything that did not refer immediately to his own state. He declared himself to have a safe and settled trust in the atonement and mediation of Christ; and he was still, as ever, fervent in his responses to prayer, strong in his friendship, and full of blessings for absent ones that were named.

In this state of calm and confident repose in the merits of the Saviour he continued till death. It was evident to those who knew him intimately, and heard him speak minutely of the symptoms of his soul, that he watched its moods and exercises very carefully, as it approached nearer and nearer the eternal world. He had spent his long life of service in the Church, and had preached to others the supports and comforts of religion for death; and he waited now to see how it would be with himself. A man of his seriousness, thought, and reflection, could not descend inconsiderately towards the gates of the grave; and his own deep sense of unworthiness prevented him from cherishing the expectation of a triumphant end. With the thorough humility of a large and reflective mind, he seemed to view the weight of glory which is sometimes vouchsafed to the dying Christian, as being beyond what he ought to think of, or pray for, as a triumph to be realized in his own personal experience. Hence he said to a friend, "My prayer is, that a life of mercy may be crowned, I will not say with a triumphant, but with a *peaceful* end." At another time, he expressed the wish of the poet of Methodism as his own, that he might "catch a look from Christ," and then "drop into eternity." His prayer was answered: his wish was realized. He had, at the end of life, peace: Christ did look upon him as he passed into eternity.

The Rev. William M. Bunting has supplied us with full evidence of this, in the very beautiful and minute memorial of his father's last years, which was read by Dr. Hannah at the close of a funeral sermon preached for Dr. Bunting, the other Sabbath, before the family in Islington Chapel. Mr. William M. Bunting relates that when, in the winter of 1856, he was summoned to his father's house, because of an alarming seizure which threatened death, his father said to him, "Well, William, I want to tell you that when I was seized the other day with that which probably was premonitory of my end, I felt no panic,—through mercy, no panic; but I felt, and feel, that it is a very solemn thing to die." His sensitively meek and lowly mind, however, shrunk from the least danger of self-confidence in connection with the saying, guarded as it was; for the next morning, when Mr. William was departing for home, the father had his son recalled to his room, and thus anxiously referred to what he had said on the preceding day: "I have been uneasy lest, in what I said to you last evening of my comfortable state of mind, I should have spoken in any degree boastfully......I wish you to understand," he added, with emphasis, "that my only rest, my only hope, is in the mercy of God through Christ."

His emotional experience was undoubtedly affected—and that considerably—by his severe and wearisome bodily afflictions and infirmities. For months before his death, he ate his food with great difficulty: and he was unable, from the failure of physical organs, to take as much nutriment as his bodily constitution required. His sleep, too, was very much broken; and both by day and night he suffered, almost unceasingly, the most irritating and acute pains from tic doloureux and from rheumatism. And as might be expected, the mind—sympathizing with the body in its sufferings, and groaning under the burden of the falling tabernacle—sometimes sank down into pensive seriousness and depressing reflections. But in all that he had to endure, he held fast his confidence in the saving mercy of God to him through Jesus Christ, though it was, as Fletcher has expressed it, by "naked faith in a naked promise." In doing this, he proved his mature strength as a Christian believer; illustrated in himself the great doctrine of salvation through faith alone which he had so perseveringly preached; and became an encouraging example to those saints of God who have not in their afflictions as much of the sensible enjoyment of religion as they could desire. His experience in death was, in fact, the solemn and impressive "Amen," which consistently terminated the principle and profession of his Christian life. It was that of entire renunciation of all reliance upon the works of the law for justification, and of pure, simple faith in the Lord Jesus Christ for salvation. Hence to Mr. William M. Bunting he remarked, after an observation had been made upon his patient endurance of affliction, "I have nothing but 'a naked faith.' There is danger in the doctrine of a naked faith,—but it is my experience. I hope I am right." And on his son assuring him that he was right, and proceeding to remind him how the Divine Atonement, and simple trust in it, magnified the law and made it honourable, while reliance upon works lowered and dishonoured it, he replied quickly, "O, as to *that*," (referring to reliance upon works,) "I never give place to it for a moment: it is a hopeless delusion." Afterwards, when spoken to by the same dear relative on his state of spiritual feeling, he answered, "I have no enjoyment but in an obstinate faith—only in an obstinate faith," he repeated with serious emphasis. To his second son, Mr. Percival Bunting, who, on approaching his bed-side, observed, "You are very ill, Father, but I hope that your mind is composed;" he responded, "Yes, but it is the tranquillity of faith, and nothing more." When Mrs. Bunting, who, with his only surviving daughter, Miss Emma Bunting, had ministered to him so tenderly during his last years of increasing infirmities, had read as far as that part of the hymn in the Supplement where the line occurs,—

"Simply to Thy cross I cling,"—

he remarked, "That is just my state of mind."

And when the "fight of faith" was over, and he knew that the victory was won, still his trust was avowedly in the mercy of God to him as a penitent sinner believing in Christ; for then he remarked solemnly, "I am a sinner saved by grace."

During the last week of his life he experienced more of the peace and joy of believing. The violence of his bodily pains had subsided, and his soul, after its severe conflict, lay becalmed in the bosom of its Divine Saviour, realizing the truth, that "they who believe do enter into rest." He was no longer able to sit up in his chair, but sank exhausted through the extreme heat of the season in his bed, as if ready to fall asleep in Jesus at any moment. He spoke but at intervals, and that faintly. He dozed at times upon his pillow; and as he woke up from soft, refreshing slumbers, he smiled upon the friends watching around him,—expressed by his looks from one to the other his loving recognition of their presence,—and then, with eyes uplifted to heaven, invoked the Divine blessing upon them. Indeed, that last week of his life on earth is described by his family as one of "sabbatic" and heavenly peacefulness; and his death-chamber is spoken of by those who were privileged to enter it, as being consciously to them "none other than the house of God and the gate of heaven." A Divine sacredness seemed to pervade and fill it; and, amidst the supernatural serenity of the place, there were thoughts not of terror, nor hardly of sorrow, but of angelic "watchers," who, with viewless forms and noiseless wings, were thronging the scene, and waiting to convey their precious charge to Abraham's bosom. His words were few, but they were confident and even joyous. At the beginning of the week he had sent for his eldest son; and said that he had "repose in a passive faith." And when, in consideration of the bodily weakness and pains which had weighed down his spirit and prevented lively exercises, that son suggested to him that he could love Jesus now, and praise Him when he should get to heaven, he answered instantly, "I can praise Him now." When his devoted daughter inquiringly observed to her father, "You are quite happy?" he replied earnestly, "Yes: peaceful and perfectly satisfied. My anchor is surely cast within the vail." To his oldest friend, the Rev. Thomas Jackson, who approached his bed with the cheering words, "Covenant mercies! everlasting mercies! mercies sealed to you by the precious blood of Christ!" he responded as loudly as possible with his failing voice, "Whose glorious mercies never end!" And when Mr. Jackson departed from him on that day, he whispered emphatically to his friend, "Perfect peace!" Two days afterwards, Mr. Jackson visited him again, and descanted on the theme of a free salvation and the sympathy of Christ with suffering saints; and the doctor, whose voice was becoming every hour weaker and weaker, exclaimed distinctly and fervently, "It is glorious!" His prayer for a peaceful end was answered, and more than answered. The Captain of his salvation did smile upon him as he went down alone into the valley to meet the last enemy. Rising from calm tranquillity and passive faith into holy exultation, he exclaimed, in the hearing of his medical attendant, Mr. Buxton, "I have fought a good fight." And when on the failure of his voice that Christian friend quoted for him the remaining words,—"I have finished my course, I have kept the faith; henceforth there is laid up for me a crown of righteousness, which the Lord, the righteous Judge, shall give me at that day," his face beamed with the radiance of grateful and joyous triumph. So that, most appropriately, he who now represents his father's honoured name in the Methodist ministry, breathed into the ear of the departing Christian conqueror the exultant words, "Victory, victory, through the blood of the Lamb!" "He fell on sleep" in death, at noon of Wednesday, June 16th, 1858.

His FUNERAL took place at the City Road Chapel burial-ground, on the Tuesday following his death, June 22nd; and was truly solemn and impressive in its circumstances. Some time before he died, he requested that whenever his funeral might occur, it might be plain and private. He also strictly enjoined that the funeral expenses might be defrayed out of his own means, and not from any public funds of the Connexion. But while, by resolute adherence to his injunction as to the defrayment of expenses, the family buried him themselves, yet a private funeral for one so largely beloved and honoured in Methodism could not be had. Friends and brethren came spontaneously from all parts of the kingdom to attend it. Committees with which he had been associated arranged to meet and attend his remains to the grave. The most honourable representatives were appointed by the Committees of the Evangelical Alliance, the British and Foreign Bible Society, and the Church, London, Baptist, and Moravian Missionary Societies, to take their places in the funeral procession. The more wealthy of the London Methodists followed voluntarily in their own private carriages the sixteen mourning coaches of the family and invited friends; while the middle classes and the poor of our people thronged the avenues and square around the doctor's house at Pentonville; lined the sides of the long thoroughfare of City Road; and filled the chapel, and its yard in front. One hundred and fifty ministers and influential laymen of the Methodist body, walking in pairs, met the funeral *cortège* on its way from Myddelton Square; and then, turning, preceded it to the burial-ground: so that the funeral, in its long line of mourners, and multitude of saddened attendants, produced a sensation even in busy London itself, and of necessity became public.

The Rev. Dr. Hannah received the body at the chapel-door, and read, in solemn and impressive tones, as it was borne up the aisle, the introductory sentences from the Burial Service of the Church of England, while hundreds of eyes began to fill with tears. The corpse was preceded by the officiating ministers,—all of whom are, more or less, white with age,—and was placed, with its dark pall, higher than the pews, in front of the monument to the doctor's friend,—Richard Watson. The seats in the lower part of the chapel were occupied by the family, the invited friends of the deceased, and the official mourners; while the enormous crowd, clothed voluntarily in mourning, filled the gallery, the staircases, and the aisles. Dr. Hannah read, from the pulpit, the proper Psalms and Lesson for the occasion,—the Rev. John Farrar, Superintendent of the City Road Circuit, leading the responses from the reading-desk below. The Rev. John Bowers then ascended the pulpit, and, after giving out two verses of an appropriate hymn, offered an earnest and comprehensive prayer. The Rev. John Scott next delivered an address on the character of the deceased,—marked by that acute analysis and wise simplicity and religious tone which distinguish his addresses. Afterwards, the venerable Dr. Leifchild, with his snow-white head, ascended the pulpit, and gave out, with deep and tremulous emotion,—

"When from flesh the spirit freed,
Hastens homeward to return,
Mortals cry, 'A man is dead!'
Angels sing, 'A child is born!'

"Born into the world above,
They our happy brother greet;
Bear him to the throne of love,
Place him at the Saviour's feet!

"Jesus smiles, and says, 'Well done,
Good and faithful servant thou!
Enter, and receive thy crown!
Reign with Me triumphant now!'"

Words cannot describe the thrilling and mingled emotion of love, sadness, joy, and spiritual exultation, with which these beautiful lines were sung by that crowded assembly. And when the minister of almost fourscore years spoke, from the pulpit, with a gushing heart and a countenance kindled into radiant expression, of his own personal remembrances of his long-known friend,—of his blooming hope of their soon meeting again in heaven,—and exclaimed with fervour, "O, joyous meeting!" hundreds burst into happy weeping, and sobbed out their feelings aloud. The Rev. John Farrar then gave out the last two verses of the New Year's hymn, commencing, "O that each in the day," &c.: after which, the Rev. Dr. Dixon, with his fine classic head also crowned with "the glory of old age," entered the black-draped reading-desk; and, with his lustrous but, alas! in late years, sightless eye-balls raised to heaven, offered, with the visions of anticipated glory fresh upon his kindling soul, the concluding prayer.

The bodily remains of the beloved and departed one were then (after some three hours' service in the chapel) slowly borne down the aisle to their last resting-place, and committed to the deep family vault at the entrance of the graveyard, by the Rev. Dr. Hoole. And when Mr. Farmer, leaning for support on the arm of the Incumbent of Clerkenwell, (the Rev. R. Maguire,) drew near to the grave, and cast into it dust from the ground's surface to mingle with the precious dust below, strong emotions were felt by all who thronged that solemn and farewell scene. Heavy with sorrowful feeling, the multitude slowly dispersed, each ready to say to the gazing persons he passed at the outer gate of the chapel-yard, "Know ye not that there is a prince and a great man fallen this day in Israel?"

It had been the long-cherished desire of Dr. Bunting to be interred, at his death, in the burial ground of City Road Chapel, where rest in solemn sepulture the bodies of Wesley, Bradburn, Benson, Clarke, Watson, and others of the mighty dead in Methodism; and for this object he had, at his first wife's death, in 1835, provided there a family vault and tomb. The sanitary laws had since closed that crowded graveyard. But, greatly to the doctor's relief, the Home Secretary, on being memorialized some months previously, had considerately granted a special licence for his interment there; so that after he had "served his generation by the will of God, and had fallen asleep, he was laid to his fathers." The signs of mourning for his death have spread throughout the land. Many of the pulpits in Methodism are now clothed in black. Funeral sermons have been preached for him in London, by the Rev. Thomas Jackson and Dr. Hannah; and in most of the cities and towns of the kingdom his death has been improved by his ministerial brethren. "He, being dead, yet speaketh!" and his remembered example of consecrated activity and energy enjoins upon us to "work while it is called to-day!"

LONDON:—PRINTED BY WILLIAM NICHOLS, 32, LONDON-WALL.

CPSIA information can be obtained
at www.ICGtesting.com
Printed in the USA
LVHW100734070123
736480LV00010B/257

9 783375 126698